"You never know what is enough, until you know what is more than enough."

— William Blake
MARRIAGE OF HEAVEN AND HELL (1793)

INDULGENCE OR GRATIFICATIONS

TALES OF TEMPTATION

AND

ONE STEP TOO FAR

FLIGHTBOOKS™ – VOLUME III

"Dangerous Dreams of Dr. Ironicus"

RENÉ BLANCO

Please accept my best wishes
for your health and happiness!
Enjoy this fun book, you'll be
rewarded many times over!

René Blanco

INDULGENCE
OR
GRATIFICATIONS
TALES OF TEMPTATION & ONE STEP TOO FAR

FLIGHTBOOKS™ – VOLUME III

Daring Dreams of Dr. Ironicus

Published by *FLIGHTBOOKS™*

For information, please contact: *FLIGHTBOOKS™ ENTERTAINMENT*

flightbooks@gmail.com

www.reneblanco.net

ISBN-13: 978-0-9834147-0-4

E-BOOK ISBN: 978-0-9834147-3-5

LCCN Library of Congress Control Number: 2020923663

FlightBooks™

Ocean Ridge, Florida

Printed in the United States of America

DEDICATED TO MY COUSIN AND
CHILDHOOD WRITING PARTNER, PAT,
WHO RARELY IF EVER FELL VICTIM TO A
TEMPTATION, OR TOOK ONE STEP TOO FAR.

STEPS TO ENLIGHTENMENT

"Open up your mind, let your fantasies unwind!"

The Phantom (of the Opera)

Contents

List of Illustrations

Foreword

by

Dr. Charles E. Vernoff

Where traditional religious worship intends for believers to create and share lofty goals, the "satanic" vision of man's ultimate purpose is simply to satiate desires through pleasure seeking, and unfettered indulgences. As if a "devilish" entity seized upon human freedom and cancels the ability to choose good, it ignores most standards of self-control, productivity, and sacrifice. That drive to push the limits of indulgence for indulgence's sake, and to satisfy evermore risky desires, has been called the satanic model of living, and is epitomized by a quotation of Aleister Crowley's, "Do what thou wilt."

If familiar support systems desert us when we are most confused or vulnerable, we might well be tempted to fall back on a devil's power because it is a way we could manage our fears or uncertainty into something that may feel better. And one thing separating man from other animals is an expanded conciousness accessible through the ingestion of substances, communing body and spirit with god-like entities from our universe by their different mood-altering and hallucinogenic properties. Then, contemplating all the extraordinary states of being afforded by these new visions of reality, and thinking. The God-entity—our concept, if you will, of gods and there being a separate Super-entity we called God who embodies enlightenment itself—is probably not "Something Other" as much as a heightened state of being in this reality of ours, a more encompassing spectrum of existing reality; like visible light which is only 10% of the entire light spectrum, so is the physical reality we can see and feel just a fraction of what is known to exist, hard as that is to conceive! Some substances are said to aid in our perceptions of these heightened realities or the broader spectrum, and provide another portal to what we know of as, and named the spirit world.

Systems of worship keep springing up around countless perceived portals to the supernatural. And, key to any system of worship which will endure is uniting their populations for common causes under shared symbols, beliefs and practices. But, so often, especially since the time of Christ, competing paths to salvation like enlightenment by or through substance use or its satanic equivalents, were deemed heretical. Rituals and customs associated with indulgence since the prehistoric times, chief among them being the ingestion of substances, conflicts with Christian-Muslim theology at the fundamental level where indulgence in higher states of being might be one of the biggest threats to highly-organized religions. When so many alternative roads to enlightenment and salvation exist, Jesus and Allah stand as two of the most jealous and dare we say, selfish children of God.

Faith in Christ and in the Christian-Muslim message, for whatever reasons, remains out of sync with pleasures of the body. They supposedly violate the principle where reliance on anything but blind faith in Christ/Allah for salvation of one's soul, is a sin worthy of eternal suffering. Naturally, this precept is rooted in the religions' desire to keep strict control of followers by preventing other avenues of feeling good or reaching salvation, so banning substances along with rituals, symbols, writings, customs, dancing, etc., practiced in those mystery religions exists to this day and still is representative of purity and piety for those who would feel threatened by a guilty pleasure. Those for whom self-denial is their ultimate expression of spiritual worthiness, propagating a belief that taking natural healing substances is shameful and immoral, then stigmatizing it further by anchoring the satanism label to its meaning, is the logical way to make everything about it antithetical to Christian values or the light of Christ. In effect, power of salvation is hijacked and perverted through devices like the so-called "indulgence" which, given one's generous contribution to their church, believers could "buy down" the amount of suffering yet to be endured in Purgatory, and gain faster admission to Paradise.

That sets the stage for these four stories about indulgent behaviors and our curious affinity for compulsively repeating them. When we are tempted and want a desire to be gratified, it is in one of three ways—our body craves something which we've probably been taught we're not supposed to have; our mind craves something we probably learned it's not supposed to have; our ego (prideful self) craves some power or a status believed necessary, but also should not be indulged. Revealed are the inherent spiritual and moral conflicts, their conditional natures plus the unique resolutions reached by the characters, allowing for a measure of enlightenment. Revelations, greed, lust and obsessions, hedonism and temptations are played out with equal thoroughness and clarity while conveying essential truths about our living in a hugely entertaining new way!

Charles E. Vernoff, Ph.D.
West Hollywood, California

Professor Emeritus, Charles Vernoff of Cornell College, is best known for "MYSTICISM: EAST AND WEST," *along with,* "CONTEMPORARY JEWISH LITERATURE," *plus,* "A HISTORY AND THEOLOGY OF THE HOLOCAUST." *Dr. Vernoff is also a religious scholar whose works have appeared in* The Journal of the American Academy of Religion, Jewish Civilization: Essays and Studies, The Journal of Ecumenical Studies, *and many other publications.*

Dr. Vernoff did his undergraduate studies at the University of Chicago, graduate studies at Harvard University, and earned his Ph.D. at the University of California, Santa Barbara.

Preface

*T*hird in the *FlightBooks* fast fiction series, *INDULGENCE OR GRATIFICATIONS* concerns people pushing personal, moral or sexual boundaries, be they real or imagined, and in doing so collectively exploring our own greater spiritual and emotional limits plus our unseen connections to the universe. Gratifying desires and excesses as much as possible without going over that "tipping point" where all would be lost, and failing to some degree, is central to the journeys or struggles of people portrayed in these pieces, as in throughout history. Their conflicts depict the unconscious motivations that have forever driven humans forward, the primal dynamics of risk vs. reward which underpins the choices we make—revealed and rendered in such terms by these humans navigating their journeys. Exactly how far can you lean out a window before finally falling out? In one context or another, that's a question we ask ourselves daily, often several times, and it guides our decision-making even if it's to avoid the window altogether!

Naturally, everyday living requires behavior conforming to the demands of a society where life resembles a balancing act of meeting our needs and commitments, while struggling with how to just feel as good as possible through it all. Each decision we weigh consciously or unconsciously against the ratios of risk-reward-loss related to choosing one alternative over another; and, should a choice be immoral and/or illegal, humans apply a secondary cost-benefit analysis around more severe penalties and risks of loss that go with über-hazardous or illegal choices. In the compulsive state, though, effective analysis is missing.

While the meaning of indulgence is yielding to a desire or temptation, the *satisfaction* and pleasing of a desire, sense or appetite, is its gratification. Indulgence is neither bad nor wrong, except when the indulging skips over its satisfaction (gratification) as can easily occur with gambling, overeating, drug addiction, crime or other risky activity, until it becomes an end in itself. If the goal is no longer pleasing, satisfaction or enjoyment of our desires, the condition rises to yet another level—that of compulsion.

Indulgence without a corresponding satisfaction doesn't just lose connection with its purpose, it can't afford satiation of any desire except through repetition of the act(s), and with little or no thought in mind but that. The sole gratification is derived from the doing of it—mindlessly repeating the risky action(s) until at some point they convert into an obligation to one's own well-being—even to one's very survival in the full-blown compulsive state. These characters also exhibit a weakness for all forms of temptation, e.g., egoism, hedonism and materialism, each of them to varying extents. So, while the stories are about realizing the limits of behavior but not exceeding them in ourselves, going straight "to the edge" and over it, does provide for the extra measure of understanding needed by most people in these stories.

Acknowledgements

The author wishes to thank the following people for something known or not, which recalls a happy feeling in recent challenging times, and for their specialness in the grander scheme of things!

Krinny McNoodle, Neil McReady, Jenna Gough, Julia Fradkin, Emma Kolbrenner, Heather LaCroix, Flor and Fidel Portillo, Daniel Weber, Lou Caplan, Spencer Sax, Clara Garcia, Robert Gemek, Hillary Paul, Liza Jane, Julie Connell, Richard and Judy Bichko, Sherri Berg, Tobi Schwartz, Niki Mercedes, Daniel Hartwell and Kerri Smith, Grant Skallerud and Evan Skallerud, Alison McCarty, Niki Lane, Magnolia Frangipani, Robert, Annette and Cassie Milton, Jennifer Sneeden, Carl and Heidi Moss, Lonnie Avant, Nick Pizzi, Danny Bled, Kristen Ann Hanson, Robert Frost, Brady Brugge, Winston Norway, Charles and Donna Edwards, Terry and Pat Curtin, Terry Passanisi, Billy Charles, Chris Riley, Bob Arabia, Alina Blanco, Phillip Salzinger, Skye Paige, Suyapa Portillo, Tim Vaughn, Charles and Donna Edwards, Barry Apfel, Carlos and Jipsy "Nefarious Girl" Castillo, Mary Ann Bittal, Jane Donoghue, Woody Flowers, Jeff Ireland.

Contributors

Sonja Karian deBlanco and Ernesto Enrique Joaquín Blanco, Sharon Ruth Ford, Charles Vernoff, Emily Teperman Rosen, John and Nvart (Rose) Karian, Grace Karian, Charles and Anne Karian, Adam, Hector and Dee Acevedo, Laurence Gartel, Crystal Lemon, Deborah Salant, Diana, Joel and Dagny Davis, Karina, Michael, Keila and Noah Baril, Elizabeth, Paulina, Nathan and David Naranjo, Ricardo, Isabela and Ana Blanco, Michael Coleman, Angel Li Causi, John Burke, Robert and Louis "Chip" Bachrach, Vicki Myers, Charles Joseph, Jon Foster, Danny Holland, Rik Thayer, Bill Stobaugh, Stephen Hanson, Tom and Lori Magno, Andrew James Casner, Cheryl Brodsky, Bob Croke, Carl and Karen Dawson, Sandy Starr, Storer Hastings and Carolyn Rowley, Scott Thorne, Randall Holton, Teva BenShlomo, Janet and Tom Pratt, Andrea Howard, Lisa Federman, Huntington Faxon Willard, Sinclair Weeks, Robett Harry Welch, Gary Joyal, Bob and Lucinda Harrison.

Marcela DiSanto: Cover Model
Laurence Gartel: Cover Art
Sharon Ford: Back Cover Art
Scott Grossberg: "Masks of Wisdom" illustration
William Blake: *Frontispiece,* "Jacob's Ladder" A/K/A "Steps to Enlightenment"

Introduction

by

Emily Rosen, M.A., M.S.

*I*NDULGENCE OR GRATIFICATIONS kicks off with a light-middleweight champion tale about money, love and one child's irresistible temptations, "Johnny Rebel Union," then it builds to a middleweight champion story of compulsion and gratification, "Higher and Higher," plus a light-heavyweight winner about anxiety and obsessing, "Diving for Dope," and concludes with an undisputed heavyweight champ about the vagaries of loving and living life shouted out loud, "Tender Concrete." These are fast, exciting stories featuring over-the-moon rich language, well-developed challenges and authentic quests for self or meaning. All revolve around taking extreme personal risks with their ramifications and trade-offs.

While not such happy endings in the sense of ecstasy or joy, these stories are triumphs of emotional satisfaction and entertainment value, testaments to making better life choices. Thus, the endings are most fitting.

Blanco's description of events as well as the dialogue are wonderfully rendered and vibrant, portraying only significant sensations for the reader. Any difference between what actual events look or sound like and their depictions, feels seamless. The prose has multiple layers of subtext which almost fly off the pages and press buttons in our heads. Each word propels the story ahead through its own energy, infusing the past with more meaning, and the future with curious intrigue, signature elements of Blanco's *FlightBooks™* series.

In addition to authoring acclaim-winning stories, novels and screenplays, Blanco is a psychotherapist and contributes to a variety of publications. His natural insights and empathy grant the characters great depth to navigate events and realize their unique destinies. Yet the style is so crisp and transparent the words almost read themselves!

Boca Raton, Florida
12:30 p.m., January 6, 2022

Besides prominent careers at major advertising and publishing houses, Emily Teperman Rosen, is best known for her decades-long freelance column, "Everything's Coming Up Rosen," and for founding the so-called "Boca School of Writing," with her famous series of workshops, "MILESTONES, MEMORIES AND MEMOIRS." She devotes much of her time to numerous charities and edits a stirring series of compilations contributed by writing students over some thirty years of teaching; they are drawn from a century of experience by many of those who have lived the past eighty, ninety or one hundred years, and still do talk about it!

Ms. Rosen received her degrees in Journalism and Education from New York University. She earned another Master's degree in Mental Health Counseling from Fordham University.

JOHNNY
REBEL UNION

(Between the States)

A child steals some money and doesn't stop.

*A*ll day Johnny was thinking about his baseball glove, about its oldness and badness and how much better he could play with a new one like he saw in the PLAYTIME store for $44.99, with the deep-trap pocket. But, Dad was angry at him for fooling around. He'd say "No!" like nothing, and he wouldn't forget either, which meant no glove for a long time.

"Jose Alvarez will surely beat me out for second base by then," he told himself. "You need that new glove, more than anything, ever."

Johnny had a good idea about his Grandpa, though. If he charged Grandpa $10 for every kiss he gave him, five kisses would be enough to buy his new glove! Still, it was horrible, those stiff greasy whiskers scraping his face, plus the old-guy smell. Eww! He hated that. Although he'd do it. Sometimes Grandad tried to get more than his money's worth by holding him tight, and planting a big gooey one. But that cost another five bucks. For the whole 45 bucks, he'd let him. Definitely.

He couldn't wait to say something at dinner. "When are we going to Grandpa's this weekend?"

"Next month," Dad answered, not looking up from the papers he was reading. He sounded a litttle angry, too. Next month was forever. There was only a few months of baseball in the whole year.

"Why do you want to know?" Mom asked. "You don't talk to your grandparents when you're there."

"I talk." Johnny tried to think of what he liked about Grandpa's. "I like driving late at night, and also stopping for a hamburger. Can't we go this weekend?"

"Your father has to work Saturday," she replied. "But that reminds me, we're going to the Coffman wedding in the afternoon. You are invited, too, you know," she told Johnny. "They have children your age."

"Coffmans?" Dad's voice went way up. "Oh noo-o! No darn-nit! I told Percy I'd work all day!" Now he was angry.

"But, you knew Ari's boy was getting married, why?"

"I forgot, Dolly, that's all."

"But, Henry…"

"Dolly, please. Okay? Percy asked me. I forgot, I didn't think. That's all." Dad was moving his food around the plate, clinking his fork. "Did you buy something?"

"Well," she said, getting up from the table. "I thought of picking up one of those gifts they reserved at Macy's." She looked in Johnny's direction. "Would you like to go with me to Macy's?"

"No, thanks… Why don't Grandma and Grandpa ever come over here? I don't want to go to the Coffman's, either."

"Nobody's forcing you to go."

"Yeah, but I wanna go to Gramma's."

"You heard what your father said."

Then there was a huge explosion—Dad's fist slamming down on the table! "Darn-nit!" he thundered. "He just wants money to buy a thing, Dolly! That's all! Whatever he wants, do not give it to him, is that clear?" Mom didn't answer right away. "Okay, Dolly?" he repeated louder.

"Yes."

Johnny stayed frozen in shock and shame.

"Whatever it is this time, little Johnny-boy…" Pointing his big finger. "You're not gonna get it. Nope. No matter how much you beg, wheedle or cry. Not this time." Now he was glad. "So just forget about it." He picked up and threw down his napkin in the exact same place "I had enough now, let's have no more arguing at the table. Dolly, please, come now, please…sit down. Come on," he told her.

"Can I be excused?" asked Johnny, desperate to go away in case he cried.

"Yes," Dad answered, all happy with himself.

So, Johnny left the table thinking of one thing—how he was going to get that glove. There was never a time when he couldn't figure out some way to get what he wanted. Maybe he could get Auntie Grace or even Uncle Stan. Except Dad would be angrier if he wheedled them behind his back now. There must be a way without him finding out ever. This was terrible. He couldn't think of anybody. Or anything. Johnny wished he could buy it alone, and show him! He was so mad at Dad for this! He felt like having a war with him. If they'd buy a gift for the Coffman's, why not him?

Johnny stopped in the upstairs hallway, listening to them argue about his job. Just because he had the money he wasn't so big. It was only 45 lousy bucks. If he had his own money he wouldn't even need them. Then, Johnny decided he didn't want their money. He would mow lawns. No… He couldn't, either. Freddie Pomeroy tried, and the older kids beat him up so he wouldn't cut in. They'd do it to Johnny in a second. At that moment he hated his father, hated Dad for trapping him this way. He wished that he was alone, on his own, free from having to ask for his things. But, Dad's voice downstairs was big and loud, like a thick hot blanket around him smothering his life. Johnny got all fired up inside and he wanted to punch something hard. The wall. He flexed his fist at a place on the wall, he was about to hit the wall and then…then, he held up, noticing the door of his parent's bedroom down the hall. For some reason he thought of going in. They were still arguing in the dining room. Johnny hardly thought more about it, but then he opened their door and went inside the bedroom.

It was cool inside, and smelled fresh. Right on top of the bureau was Mom's pocketbook. It was the first thing he saw! He moved there, as if being pulled, his heart pumping in his stomach. What in the world was he thinking about? Stealing? Yes…he was thinking about it. He pecked at the clasp of the pocketbook, then went back near the door… Still arguing… He returned to the bureau and pressed on the clasp. It popped wide open! Back to the door again… Still arguing. Then right back over to the pocketbook. He plunged into envelopes and brushes and keys jingled while the sweet smell of lipstick or perfume got him dizzy. Then, he saw money in an envelope! Right near the top!

This was all perfect, as if God wanted Johnny to have his glove even if Dad didn't. It seemed so easy, and good like a miracle happening. Or was this temptation but the devil was behind it instead? He wondered if a devil could do miracles too. So Johnny whirled around, and began throwing punches behind him, punching the air with all his might, where he can almost feel a devil dodging and weaving, but not going away.

Suddenly, everything had turned silent. No more voices! He jumped to the door. They stopped arguing! He went crazy in fright! He'd be caught here with Mom's pocketbook open!

His heart thumped loud enough to hear. Then, Mom said something. Dad said something else before things went silent again. He prayed they weren't coming upstairs for anything. But, Dad started talking, explaining a lot. He kept talking and talking. Mom said stuff, too. Oh! Thank You, God! he almost blurted out loud! He was still okay.

Back again to the envelope with the money—a hundred. A hundred, one hundred! It was full of new $100 bills! There was so much! Much more than he needed, or dreamed! Only hundred dollar bills, though. First, he looked all around him, almost sure someone was watching. But, not even that would stop him now. Devil or not Johnny had to take one of the bills since there was nothing else. They had so much more money than he dreamed. And, giving him such a fight when it was most important to play his best. This was a terrible thing. But he was doing it anyway… He convinced himself it was done as his fingers pulled free a hundred dollars. The corners were stiff as knife points, and the edges razor sharp. Was the old glove really so bad? He should check it again. Except, there was all the money, as if waiting for him… But, it still wasn't right. Unless…unless maybe God wanted Johnny to get the glove and beat out Jose Alvarez, but this was the only way God could make it happen. That was also possible.

It was like jumping off a cliff when he finally stuffed a $100 bill into his pocket. There was a crackle sound as it got crushed down to a many-pointed ball in his pants. Now there was no putting it back. Pretty fast he put everything else like before, and the purse clinked when it closed.

Johnny sneaked into the hall with the sharp-pointed bill scratching the inside of his leg, and he felt free, he did. He'd buy his glove, and return the change, they would never know.

Dad was still talking, not loud, though. He could tell they weren't arguing anymore. So, he went to his bedroom, hardly able to catch his breath, shaking in terror and excitement and relief that he made it without getting caught. He could only dream about his new glove, every few minutes taking out the money to look at, and smell it. This was the biggest thing he ever tried, the bravest thing he ever did. Mom would get it all back. They would have their money. And he would have his glove. They'd be even.

Johnny woke up way before Mom and Dad which never happened before. And, after school he walked slowly over to the PLAYTIME store, trying to make his excitement go longer and wondering what else he could have with the extra $50.

Maybe he shouldn't put back $50 since he took a whole $100, Mom would know right away. Out loud, he said, "No.

I won't spend the other $50."

At last, Johnny was there! A little bell clanged above his head when the door opened, and a tall skinny man with thick glasses looked over.

"Hi," said Johnny.

"Well, Hi there to you!" said the man. "You look happy."

"I am! Buying my new glove."

"The one you were looking at before?"

"Yeah. You didn't sell it to someone else, did you?"

"As a matter of fact…" he said, walking quickly over to the gloves. "We had a fine young fellow try it on this morning. Let's see… No, here it is."

"Yeah! That's my glove!" Johnny grabbed it to punch in the pocket again and again.

"Mighty fine glove. Definitely worth all of $49.99." The tall man walked behind the counter. "Plus your tax."

"Forty-nine ninety-nine?" Johnny was surprised about it costing more than he thought. Now he couldn't put back the other $50 anyway. "Oh, well, with this new glove I'll beat out Jose Alvarez for second base, no problem."

"You bet, son. So, will there be anything else?" he said, taking the money.

"Anything else?" Johnny repeated.

The man's glasses were big and thick, and his eyes were little blue dots behind them. "Sure. How about saddle soap? You need the saddle soap to break it in right, " he told Johnny. "It's no good without your soap."

"Saddle soap?" Johnny wondered. His eyes went around the room, toys hanging from the ceiling, stacked on shelves, piled on the floor, all colors and chrome, shiny boxes, trains, planes, anything he wanted. Plus his glove!

The tall clerk was real nice, he showed Johnny just how to break in the glove. Then he bought a Barry Bonds bat, plus a Roger Clemens baseball. Johnny was happy with his $100 worth. He'd repay it somehow. For the rest of the afternoon he played running-the-bases with Freddie and Eileen Small. Eileen didn't want to use the new glove but Freddie did, and Johnny had to chase him down to get it back. He also didn't use his Barry Bonds bat yet, but the Roger Clemens baseball got wicked scratched from playing in the street.

Johnny sneaked into the house and hid everything in the boiler room, except the scratched ball which he kept with his old glove. Then, he asked Mom to call him for dinner.

He ate second helpings, and later went to watch TV but his Mom was snoring at it. Dad was downstairs in his office, working on some stuff. He always worked on stuff.

Hiding in the boiler room, Johnny started breaking in his glove. It was beautiful. He compared it to his old one, and it was great, much bigger to catch everything, and real soft with the nice smell of leather. He couldn't wait for Little League. His thoughts drifted to the man at PLAYTIME, and the other things he could have had for $100. Not that he wasn't happy. He could've bought the catcher's mitt for Eileen, since she had trouble catching. And the *War Between the States* battle game was about the best toy ever, it had everything, guns that really shoot, and the bridge that blows up by remote! Johnny wanted it. Suddenly he wanted it just as bad as his glove. He could have it, too. $49. It wasn't even $100. Dad didn't come upstairs, so he checked on his mom, but she was still snoring.

Maybe if he did it now when Mom was asleep. The hall was dark and living room dim, only the TV shadows moving. Without a sound he tip-toed in the hallway, peeked down and saw his Mom shifting her position in the chair, but she didn't wake up. Johnny didn't know what these feelings were. This was so easy and he never knew. He never wanted to find out.

Before taking it, he also thought of letting Grandpa kiss him a few times and threatening to tell his mom. That must be worth at least $100. But, he wasn't sure if he could be so bad to hurt Grandpa like that. He just smelled bad, and not all the time, either. He might never get another dollar from him, or anyone else. So, he decided to save that plan, and use it as a last resort if he really, really needed something that bad.

He opened the bedroom door. There was her pocketbook again, like it hadn't moved. He dug out another $100 without disturbing anything else, doing his best to fold it only once so maybe he could put it back, then he went right to the kitchen as if wanting to cover or shower himself in its bright lights.

The next day after school, he returned to PLAYTIME. Of course, it was so exciting, and Johnny ran most of the way. The same sales clerk with big round glasses was there.

"I want that *War Between the States* game, please. But, can I buy the Lincoln Logs, and the big Stuka bomber there, and some other things if I only have a $100?"

"Well, let me see now," he answered, moving over there pretty fast. "$29.50. Plus $9.99. Hmm…" He figured, writing on a box. "And, that is $49.99…and that's $7.16 tax, so… Yes, that will fit in there very nicely, I think!" he said, sliding

Johnny's bomber off the crammed shelf.

Johnny was happy and surprised about getting everything he wanted, plus some money back! Double-good!

That same night, he took his third $100 bill, and went to sleep. He also had a strange dream—an angel and two devil-babies were playing, and wrestling in his parents' bedroom. The big devil baby wanted a donut hole which the little devil did not want to give him. So when the little devil finally fell asleep, the big devil stole his donut hole while the angel only looked up, and cried. He didn't understand it, but he did think about asking his Mom.

At PLAYTIME the following afternoon, Johnny bought paints for his new bomber, that catcher's mitt for Eileen, and even things he never thought about buying like checkers and chess, mini racing cars, a Barbie & Ken set for his cousin Pat, and another model plane. He hardly thought about the buying part anymore, there was so much money he couldn't think of what to take.

Eileen thanked him for the glove. Then, Johnny went to Freddie's and left his Lincoln Logs there, they were so heavy. He lugged the rest of his stuff to the boiler room and gazed at it like it was treasure, hidden treasure, bright and new, most things not even opened yet. Johnny loved new toys more than anything. When he picked one up, he could smell that sweet smell in PLAYTIME. He'd never forget it. Or the tall man.

After dinner Mom went to Weight Watchers, so Johnny spread out a big battle in the boiler room. He wanted to take out his new *War Between the States* but it wasn't safe. Soon he got tired of playing with the old toys and started breaking in his new mitt with saddle soap. It had a tiny cut in the deep pocket which wouldn't go away, and he thought of returning the glove. Then he punched the pocket wicked hard and loud before he needed to hide it again. But, his father showed up, asking what all the noise was about, and almost saw the new glove! So, instead, he tried to run his old trains, except there were sections of bad track. He should have remembered that today when wondering what to buy.

Mom came home, and soon she fell asleep on the couch again. Johnny said to himself, "Just one more time."

There was nothing he could think of buying, except that new track. So he decided to save the rest, just in case. It was a close call, too. He was pulling out the $100 when Dad called up the stairs for Mom. Johnny's heart jumped right up in his throat and stuck there like a big plug. But, he still made it out to his room seconds before Mom stumbled around the corner. God! That was even more scary than the first time! Suddenly, Johnny knew he couldn't do it again. He was really happy, he had everything he wanted, plus the extra $100, and didn't get caught, even if he deserved it. He also didn't feel bad about not being able to play with his toys. He thought that was fair.

He bought another glove, something like his old one, the "Lie Detector" game for cousin Pat, Iris-monster stickers for his bike, a glow-in-the-dark gyroscope and his new track. He felt so free! He didn't know where to stop and fill up his cart next! He said Good-bye to the nice man, who replied, "Good-bye!"

***

On Saturday, Johnny's parents went to the Coffman's so Freddie and Eileen came over with a new kid, Paulo. Johnny had more toys than all of them now, and he thought Freddie was angry because he left pretty fast. Then Eileen and Paulo, they left, so he wound up playing just with himself.

At last Johnny could spread out a great big *War Between the States* on the living room carpet. Rug stains made good ponds, and the holes were perfect as bomb craters. He wanted the Rebels to win but the Union guys murdered them. Rebels kept charging over the bridge, until the Yankee spy with one arm shot the Rebel general in the back, and blew the bridge, trapping the Rebel army against the wall. The Union spy was so bad Johnny wanted to torture and murder him. But his first big battle was lost. The Union freed the slaves, then burned everything which might have been okay, Johnny didn't know anymore. He wasn't happy. Not at all. He felt so strange and dumb playing war like that. It was true, he didn't know why.

Today was nothing like he expected. He had more toys, but not friends, and so many Union soldiers were killing the Rebels that Johnny knocked it all over. Then, he twisted off the spy's head, plus his good arm. Part of Johnny felt sick like something horrible eating and hitting him from the inside out. Another part of him only wanted things back how they were a few days ago. Except for his glove. Or the *War* game. He'd even give back the *War* game just to keep his glove. But if he kept the glove, why not his *War* game? He kept smelling the sweetness inside Mom's pocketbook. Then he couldn't help it, he began to cry, crying harder than he ever had. He didn't know why. He only prayed they would never know. At least if they caught him, they'd find out how bad he really was.

That moment he felt loud rumbling under the house, the grinding chain of the garage door opening! His Mom and Dad were home! He dumped his whole *War* back in the box, and slid it under the couch. Then he gathered everything else into both arms and ran them to his room, falling and kicking toys inside. He was safe for now.

Over several days Johnny was giving things away since none of his hiding places was any good. People thanked him, but they couldn't figure out why he'd buy them stuff. Johnny just told them, "Don't worry. You don't have to thank me."

He decided to keep his Lincoln Logs but Freddie wanted them so bad he was ready to fight about it, and dared Johnny to take them back. So, he gave those up, too. He never played with most of the toys but Johnny didn't mind much, his Mom never found out. She even seemed nicer to Johnny, especially after he made money washing cars in the neighborhood.

She also went to a Little League game, although he told her he probably wouldn't play. Then, leading late in the game, the coach put him in as a pinch runner. But he missed a "steal" sign, got picked off-base and trapped in a pickle before being run down, and tagged out. Still, in the final inning the coach kept him in to play second base. He made two errors because he couldn't use his new glove with Mom there, and the team lost. It was awful, the coach took Johnny off the field, and no one spoke to him after. He heard others saying how he sucked, though. And how they hated him. Maybe Mom heard, too.

Just before going home a couple teammates came up to Johnny. One clapped him on the shoulder. "Don't worry, it's just a game, shake it off."

Johnny almost felt better, until the other kid added, "Oh, yeah! Shake it off!" He began shaking and fumbling with his glove, and the ball. "Shake it off!" He kept dropping the ball, kicking it and then chasing it around in the dirt to make fun of Johnny's fielding, as more kids laughed and laughed. "Shake it off baby!" The teammate continued his herky-jerky acting until the coach finally stopped it. Johnny wasn't even mad at the kid making fun of him. He didn't want to beat him up or anything, he just felt empty, like nothing. He saw his mother and the coach, and it seemed they all thought the same thing. How could Johnny ever play again? Why would he want to?

After he had gone to bed and almost fallen asleep, Mom opened his door and asked him to come on down to the living room, which he did without thinking. He crawled up on Dad's big leather chair while his mother sat on the couch. Then, she stared right into Johnny's face, and stuck her hand under the couch. When Johnny saw that *War Between the States* slide out, his whole mouth dried up, and his throat hurt like fingers he couldn't see were squeezing hard on it. He forgot all about his *War* game! And couldn't believe he had!

"How did you get this?" she asked.

"I don't know." There were silent seconds. "What is it?"

"You know very well."

"Is it...something for me?"

"You know very well. Where did it come from, or must we get your father?" She was not going to give up. The leather chair was sticking to his back and legs and he almost couldn't move. This was no dream but he still prayed it was! His heart was beating so fast it was like just one heartbeat! "Will you answer me, how did this *thing* get under my couch?"

"I can't…right now." His brain was a blank, frozen, and locked like in a thought-prison.

His mom stood up in a flash.

"No, Mom, please. Don't get Dad. I just washed lots of cars." Johnny began to cry. "I'm sorry, I swear to God, Mom. Please, he doesn't have to know, does he? I got it a long, long time ago. At PLAYTIME. A long time ago."

She pushed out a breath.

Finally, he felt good to be crying like that. But in seconds Dad's voice came from upstairs. "Dolly, what is wrong? Are you crying?" Mom didn't answer. "Dolly, please, tell me?"

Mom looked at Johnny as if she was very sorry. She may have saved him, but he gave himself up by crying so hard that Dad heard. "Your son. He's crying."

"He is? Oh… Well…what seems to be wrong?" Pause. "Is it something important? Because, you know, I have to get up very early. And your mother does, too."

Johnny couldn't think of anything because he was crying and he couldn't let Dad see him this way. But he deserved for them to hate him. He hated himself. He wanted to die. So he wouldn't have to feel anything else, especially this.

Mom was watching Johnny, and didn't answer Dad. "I'll be right down, Dolly," he said, and the door blew closed.

She went upstairs to meet him first. Johnny stayed on the leather chair, sniffling, tasting his tears. He could not look at the *War* box. And, now Dad would see it, so the memory of his father's hand smashing the tabletop popped into his head.

What were they waiting for? If there hadn't been a *War Between the States* he wouldn't have got caught. It was junk anyway. Toys were lousy, he never wanted another. He'd give his toys to needy kids overseas, and they could play. Except his trains.

What was happening? Maybe God was saving him. No, he deserved to go to jail for this. Maybe they were calling the police! God, no, please. That would be the end, God, no!

The door cracked open upstairs. They walked in. Dad's head was down. Mom looked sideways.

Johnny cried by himself. "Did you call the police—you didn't... Did you?"

"Not yet," Dad answered. He bowed his head like he was sad, not so mad, and seemed to stare at a spot on the carpet.

"I didn't mean to do it. I didn't."

"But...why?" Mom asked. "Don't we give you enough that you shouldn't have to steal?"

"I didn't steal it. I took it."

"No..." Dad said slowly. "It wasn't yours." His voice got stronger. "You stole it."

"No. No, I just *took* it. It was like all our family things. I was going to pay it back. I swear. Really."

Dad's head went down more and stayed forward. Johnny heard him breathing hard while staring at a rug stain or hole.

"How much did you take?" asked his Mom, barely able to look at her boy.

"A hundred dollars."

"There was much more missing from my pocketbook."

"No, Mom, I'm sure, it was only $100, I know—"

"Don't you lie to me, brother!" her voice went way up. "It's hundreds—"

"Dolly, please!" Dad cut her off, then she stared straight ahead. "Son…" he began. "We are not sure you will be able to understand. It's hard to understand, why you've stolen—"

"No, I *took* it."

"No, you stole it!" He rose up and stared down hard at his son. "You took it without asking Mammy. That is stealing."

Johnny couldn't stand it. His father's eyes were like ray guns burning through him. He felt heavy and couldn't move, thinking about Dad's hand whacking the table, or his head or behind. All his skin was sticking to the leather and covered in goose bumps. Then, he saw that he was naked, naked except for his underwear, with his eeny-peeny there, and Johnny felt so nothing, so ashamed, and dirty in front of Mom and Dad. He wanted to cry again but now he couldn't even do that.

"Every crook," Dad said, "knows that stealing is wrong, but he believes he has good reasons. He believes what he did isn't so bad. That might be easier for a while, but it is no fun. He doesn't think he'll be caught. But everyone gets caught." His voice went up again. "And he goes to jail."

Dad stopped a moment while Johnny cried and sniveled. "No, son, the law is the same for everybody. What you have done is just as bad as if you had gone out and robbed a bank. But, we were the bank." His father took another deep breath, still staring ahead, and down at the floor. "Dolly…" he said, and stopped more seconds to think. "Do we call the police?"

She continued to look down and ahead, along with Dad.

Several seconds later, she replied, "Did you understand

anything your father was saying?"

"Yes," Johnny answered. "I didn't think about doing it. It wasn't worth it. You're right." He tried not to cry. "It was just there. I thought you wouldn't know."

"But, you know we always find out sooner or later." She seemed to beg her son to comprehend.

"I know. But I didn't think… Enough."

"It doesn't matter if others know," said his Dad. "You do know. You can never be happy like that, or respect yourself."

Mom was so sad that she started to cry, and his Dad got choked up, too, causing Johnny to feel more love for them.

His Dad told him, "You can't imagine how much you've hurt Mammy and me. I wish you knew. Sometimes we argue but that does not mean we don't love you. We don't give you anything you want all the time because we can't. That money was for the house. Our food, your TV. We don't exist so you get what you want when you want it. No. Although, you seem to think we owe it to you. No. Life doesn't *owe* you. Or love you or give you anything. *We* do. Only we give things to you because we love you. We love you. See?"

Johnny nodded up a little. When he realized how much they loved him, he felt worse about hurting them for a dumb baseball glove he couldn't even use, and it made Johnny love them more than he dreamed he could love, which was much more than he could ever love toys. He never understood what love meant before.

In a minute Mom made a sound like she was very tired, and spoke hopefully, "Have you learned anything from this?"

"Yes, Mom." Johnny sniveled. "Oh, Dad, I'm sorry." He

went into Dad's arms. "I'm so rotten, why do you love me?"

"No, no, you aren't rotten. It was a very bad mistake—"

"—Rotten, rotten, rotten!" he cried out.

"No, don't ever say that. You see it wasn't worth it. You are still our good boy. We love you more than anything."

"Do you really? How could you still love me?"

"We can't explain it," Dad replied. "But, we never stop loving each other because we make mistakes."

They helped Johnny feel better than he ever dreamed he could feel. He knew they loved him so much that he wanted never to make them sorry again. They promised to love each other always even if they became angry or disappointed.

Soon, Johnny asked, "What are you going to do?"

Mom glanced over at Dad. "Nothing. Make you pay it back," Dad replied. Both kept looking across the carpet when Johnny realized for the first time how stained it was.

"I'll pay it back—much more."

Mom replied, "We can talk about that tomorrow. It's a school day and now it's late. Up to bed, young man."

As she talked, Johnny also felt very sleepy, and kissed them both, then headed up to bed. But, he stopped at the top of the stairs. "Mom…"

Her head turned around. "Yes?"

"You were right. I did steal $400."

They didn't say anything, though Johnny could tell they were a little happier with him.

The End of That…

EPILOGUE

Without realizing it, Johnny had outgrown toys and war games. They were never fun to play again. Maybe the stealing ended his childhood. Or, it was a last desperate try to hold on to his childhood. Childhood was over, though.

After re-paying his parents by washing cars around the neighborhood, Mom gave Johnny his new glove for the start of next Little League season. At the end of the first practice, he hid it under the bench while he ran to the bathroom, and he returned a minute later but it was gone. Stolen. Johnny never dreamed anybody on his team could do that. It smacked him between the eyes like a screaming wicked line drive. That's how Mom and Dad must have felt.

A bunch more car washes later, he got a better glove for less money at another store. It was hopeless, though, Johnny realized he never had a prayer of beating out Jose Alvarez at second base no matter what he tried, Jose was too good. He also realized little things in life mattered as much as big ones because not knowing that one little thing at the beginning is what led to him knowing all about two of the biggest things in life—love and money!

***

The next year, playing in a new league, the other team's pitcher had a mitt that looked just like his stolen one with the deep-trap pocket. The kid wasn't on his old team, so he didn't think much of it until Johnny and his teammates bombed him off the mound and he threw his mitt in the dirt by the bench. Knowing how little things mattered as much as the big ones, Johnny decided to find out if it was his glove. Just to see. And know. His glove had a small cut in the pocket, and both boys were about the same size since it also meant risking a fight.

The teams shook hands after the game, and when Johnny shook the pitcher's hand, he said, "Hey, neat glove. I wanted that kind, but didn't find one. Can I see how you broke it in?"

The other kid thought for a second before opening it up so Johnny could see the deep-trap pocket. There was the little cut in the leather. His stolen glove! "Where did you buy it?" he asked the pitcher.

"Somebody left it on the field," he replied. "My brother picked it up so no one would steal it. Then he waited for the owner to come back, but no one did! Pretty good, huh?" He smiled. "Why, you wanna buy it?"

"Na-h. How much do you want?" Johnny thought about claiming the glove back, but he didn't really care enough to fight. Despite losing the money, he would only claim it if he wanted a fight more than the glove since he wouldn't use it, his new one was that much better. Maybe this kid's brother did take the glove so it wasn't stolen, and he waited, too, but Johnny never saw him there. Or, maybe this was the one who stole it.

"That's my lost glove," Johnny couldn't help telling him.

"Oh, yeah! Right! I bet you want me to give it back too!"

"Nah. It's cursed," said Johnny, and he smiled sincerely. "I guess that's maybe why I don't have it anymore."

The kid was surprised. Then, he looked more concerned or worried when Johnny quickly turned around, and walked away without the glove or a fight. "Hey…why is it cursed?"

But, like childhood, Johnny had enough of the glove. He saw how happy his life had been without it so he didn't want to change that! He never felt the glove was his, anyway, and believed it helped him learn about money and love, but after doing its part in Johnny's life, it was gone—doing things for a time with this kid then maybe off again to do more in other peoples' lives. Or not. Even if it rotted from never being used again, it still had its place and meaning, he could see that too! Along with Johnny himself, and the whole world of stuff, he felt like the glove and *War* game, plus what he gave up, were somehow "loaned" to him as the pieces of whatever would or wouldn't happen next, before landing in their new places to spend another while in.

He could imagine the glove and everything else being the same, moving in and around, on and through or out of other things, but never without leaving their effects along the way such as learning about love and money from it. He guessed the world was a great ball of things always touching, adding and changing itself. And nothing is wasted, either, since no "thing" had another place it should be, or would be, or other stuff it could be doing, except what it was right then!

BRIDGE THAT BLOWS UP!

HIGHER AND HIGHER

(The Palace of Wisdom)

Teenager hates her life until trying drugs, with unpredictable results.

TURNING ON

Winona "Win" Miller hated her life until she smoked some grass. It was a drone of boring meaningless activities she endured like freezing weather. Still, she didn't feel anything the one time she tried smoking pot, right before the first moon landing in 1969, and she wondered, What's all this fuss about grass?

The Woodstock Festival was less than a month later and Win's curiosity was high, but only a few classmates with cool parents got to go, and she'd never dare ask her up-tight Mom and Dad. She ran across weed now and then—a couple Black kids lit a joint in the back of a bus and another time pungent clouds filled a subway tunnel. Winnie could get the stuff but never wanted it enough to search. There was so much trouble from terrorism, race and anti-war protests, hippies or drugs, Win just wanted to go underground and escape it all.

She studied lots of math and sciences, then at the start of senior year she received a letter from M.I.T., the prestigious

Massachusetts Institute of Technology where she applied for no other reason than her father was a teacher there.

Win's mother, who was tall and skinny like her daughter, but with a larger nose, brought the envelope. "Winnie, dear… It's a letter, from M.I.T."

Mrs. Miller stood by, wringing her hands while Winnie opened it. She read the first lines without expression. Then, she continued to read.

"Well…well, what?" demanded her mother, "Bad news, they didn't accept you?"

Win spoke in disbelief, "I got in." She smirked. "Wow."

Her mother snatched the letter. "Yes, you're *in*, Winnie! You're going to M.I.T.!" She almost crushed the paper in joy and relief. "Oh, this is the best news ever! My Winnie!" she cheered. "Good Lord! Oh, my God, thank You! Thank *You!*"

To everybody's surprise, and especially hers, Win gained Early Acceptance to M.I.T., mainly because she was among the few female applicants, and her dad was a professor. Still, she didn't think much of herself. She had some so-so friends and considered herself fatally uncoordinated, never graceful or good at anything except board games, trivia, and statistics about all the things she sucked at doing.

She did not even like math and sciences, but got through them the same as she got through everything else. There was no excitement, or joy. Geometry was different, though. Who knows why, but all the shapes and the theorems fell together in her mind, and she started getting As! It was rarer still that Winnie liked anything or had a flair for it, yet she also had to admit liking geology class because the teacher turned her on,

Mr. van Beever. He was tall and smart with curly blond hair and just sailed around the world. As for other guys, forget it, she was so nervous she could hardly talk. Or think. In truth, she often blanked out. Mr. van Beever was different. They'd discuss cool new discoveries like how or why rocks change.

On New Year's Eve, Win's parents went to a party while she stayed home, feeling like her normal self, not belonging or invited anywhere. Her parents were not unhappy that she was staying home, either. But, she did have a joint of weed which was supposed to be super-good. A hippie gave it to her when she was taking out trash at her restaurant job, and just by accident she caught one of her classmates, Eve Foster, the second this bearded hippie was giving her something behind the dumpster. Both spotted Win at the same time, and froze. What looked like a crooked cigarette dropped out on the icy pavement. All three of their frosty breaths pumped fast.

"Shut-up about this, Skinny Winnie!" Eve raised her smart-aleck voice. "You'd better not tell a soul," she ordered in a vindictive tone, and scooped up the funny cigarette.

Eve wasn't one of the "cool" girls at school. In fact, she was rather *un*-cool, bad at sports, founded the bird-watching club, and played a dented French horn that always dripped saliva. Except she had an A-rating from Harvard University, meaning she was granted automatic acceptance there.

"No, I wouldn't do that," Winnie told her. Although she did not appreciate Eve calling her Skinny Winnie, she didn't complain about it. "Never thought you'd do that stuff."

"Oh, it is fantastic. You never tried any?" Her classmate had a plump freckle face, a $300 Harris Tweed overcoat and thick red hair swept across her forehead, like a turban. Just a wicked smart rich girl with not a shred of fashion sense.

"I did try some," said Win. "It sucked. Did nothing."

"No…" claimed the bearded hippie. His eyes were big, and clear blue-green. "This is the real thing. Acapulco Gold. I can also lay some trippy Honduran buds on you," he spoke in a clear soft voice, calling himself "Acid Scott," and had a cherubic face, ripped hippie jeans with colored patches, and wild mussed-up hair crowned with a halo of flower blooms.

The moment she thought about how weird Scott looked, she caught a reflection of herself in a dirty window, dragging bulging garbage bags in her soiled uniform, with a long tired face. She felt so unhappy, like she was sleepwalking through life when others swore that she had everything going for her, including wonderful parents and tremendous career of some kind waiting. Except, the path she saw ahead was more like the crooked line of dumpsters and potholes in this alleyway. Then, this Scott guy comes along with a happy twinkle in his eyes, not like he's doped up, though.

"You know what…" he told Winnie. "Here you go." He handed her a marijuana joint. "For a rainy day. Dream away." He nodded with a warm inspiring expression. His smile was also kind and sincere as though he was positive about giving her something great. A Grass Fairy, that's how he looked.

Win considered it. The air was tooth-gnashing cold, and breathing the sharp stink of garbage was like inhaling razor blades. She hoisted her garbage into the dumpster and stared hard at Eve. "You really think it's that good?"

Eve nodded emphatically. "Totally! That's super duper!"

she declared. "Remember the algorithm project we had to do, what a pain it was? That even makes algorithms fun."

Besides enthusiasm, Winnie's classmate got much better grades. If it made algorithms fun, that was almost a miracle! So, she took the joint, and put it away for a special occasion.

Now, six months after she first tried grass and didn't get high, Win brought out the marijuana cigarette on New Year's Eve, and fingered it until a few grains fell out which sparkled like diamond dust. She examined the grains with a magnifier and they were all encrusted with a fine golden fuzz similar to crystals. Unlike the first marijuana she tried, this had a spicy perfume scent which changed to thick fragrant smoke upon lighting. The aroma reminded Win of church incense. Then, after a few puffs, she began to wretch and cough violently!

Worse yet, the joint started exploding in her hand like a trick cigar! It shot fiery sparks at her face and all around the living room! The oldest joke in the world, and she falls for it!

"Grass Fairy, my ass!" she shouted at the image of Acid Scott's cherub face!

More sharp blasts shocked the life out of her! Shooting cinders flew every which way until she saw it was not a trick or joke, just marijuana seeds bursting from the heat. None of this was like her first joint! Now she expected big things! But once again, nothing happened.

What a rip-off! She lost all respect for Eve. What a fool! Throwing money away on a myth. This whole pot craze was pure hype! And, while pondering the bad information about drugs and everything else on the news, without warning her stomach gurgled and churned. Then an unstoppable surge of food clumps sprang right up into her throat, and erupted from her mouth in a spray that resembled a whale's blowhole!

"Screw this shit!" she screamed out, pressing her sleeves across her mouth to stop more rancid throw-up. In a muzzled voice she stomped around yelling, "I'm never doing that shit again! Never!"

She hustled for a rag and proceeded to mop the areas of projectile vomit on her mom's century-old Persian rug, soon realizing that she was also smiling to herself and dabbing up the mess in slow, circular motions. She pictured the sad child slaves weaving the rug. Two of them would work a couple years to weave *one* rug. No, she didn't feel so bad about her mother's prize possession, not compared to the child slaves.

Unfortunately, one century later Winnie had this strange accident on the rug. She got violently ill. But, she didn't care and laughed about Mom having to live with the knowledge it was vomited on! She wanted to see her mom's reaction, that dumb confused face showing all the disappointment she felt in Winnie. She hated that look of, You should feel so guilty for disappointing me. This would zing her tidy life! Then, she would just change to that sympathetic, suspicious edge in her voice, "But, Winnie, child, honey, what could you have been doing?" Again, Win laughed at her pathetic upset.

Suddenly, she felt almost weightless. She sensed herself being whisked up and away in a single breathtaking sensation of wonderment, some soaring excitement which knocked out her normal bored condition and this fantastical warm feeling of comfort and dreaminess overwhelmed her like the tender touch of pleasure rubbing all over. WOW!

In one unbelievable instant, Win's life switched from all grays and browns, to brilliant CinemaVision! This place felt like another familiar house in a strange new world, as if she skipped over to an exciting parallel universe that seemed so warm and pleasurable, opposite of what she knew! She flew headlong into the deepest thoughtful state of amazement and satisfaction, unlike her entire day-in-and-day-out existence.

But, she was also alert, keenly aware of every last thing around her, smells, each traffic noise outdoors, with the wind rustling trees and rattling windows, the distant rumble of the furnace pumping heat through the pipes, and a Three Stooges marathon on TV at low volume. Everything seemed fresh and crisp, all the noises, details of the furniture she touched, even the sensations of sitting here with this heightened awareness of her blood and organs inside the warm bag of flesh called Winona Miller. Living itself seemed brand new like she had emerged fully conscious from the womb into the world! This was nothing like she imagined "doped up" would be. It could be what she was missing all her life!

The grandfather clock ticked off second after second, as Winnie visualized the intricate mechanisms clicking inside it. Familiar objects seemed to glow with a fascinating aura, and wonderful feelings beyond anything she dreamed flowed all through her. She felt better than ever, tremendous, so relaxed and excited too. Perfect. Each split-second contained another awesome sensation or idea. Colorful patterns of her mother's Persian rug blended with new swirls of vomit spray, and she couldn't stop laughing about it! Her perception of all the old was changed in what she realized was minutes.

Win left a part of herself behind, her unhappy self. For the first time she *knew* she was alive, really feeling her heart pushing its life blood through her and having something else to compare with the interminable dullness of her usual state. Living was altered forever while seeing her existence from a radical new perspective that seemed so much better.

Still, she had to clean Mom's priceless rug and pictured them having an argument and coming home early to nail her! My God, how bad would it be talking to them like this? And how long would these feelings go on, she had no idea. What if she never came down from the drug? She started worrying and to feel sick again. On the news they were always talking about hippies not being able to come down from a bad drug, then going nuts! Gushes of panic juice flooded Winnie head to toe. What if she went too far over the edge already!

She bounced off the couch, peering up and around her at the windows, walls and doors with a frantic series of gloom and doom thoughts invading her mind. How was she ever to get down from here? Not that she wanted to yet. But, she had no idea what was happening to her. Plus, she only seemed to be getting higher and higher!

Win's heart raced at the possibility that she went too far. Sounds of the Stooges marathon were sharp, and the volume jumped up when the Three Blind Mice theme song started. It anchored her mind to an ancient memory while their comedy took on a radically different meaning. As a child she thought of them as stupid clowns, but here their genius for all things satirical was revealed in its glory.

Winnie laughed like mad for a solid hour, revisiting the

episodes where poverty and prejudice cause them to peddle a snake oil medicine called "Brighto!" And the one where they impersonate doctors and make every emergency worse with the intercom blaring, "Calling Doctor Howard! Doctor Fine! Doctor Howard!" Then, the episode where Moe plays Hitler, Curly is Goëring, Larry Fine is Goebbles, and they fight off Stalin, Tojo and Mussolini for possession of the toy world!

This was so much fun, it may not be that bad if Winnie never came down! Then she also felt guilt and fear because it was supposed to be bad, and wrong. Therefore, she must also be bad, which she always feared was true anyway. Now there was proof since she was enjoying these great new sensations and happy feelings.

She always believed there must be some good reason for being alive, and having feelings in the first place, so perhaps this was it for her! Now there was good reason to be excited about getting up other than doing what she was supposed to do according to Mom and Dad. Now there was something for herself, for her own happiness or feeling good.

Everything was magical on this night—even a hilarious Peter Sellers movie came on TV, *I Love You, Alice B. Toklas* about someone turning on to grass for the first time! She kept singing the title song, "I love you, Alice B. Tok-las / So does Ger-trude Stein / I love you, Alice B. Tok-las / Gonna change your name to mine!"

Before her parents returned home, Win accidentally ran across the marijuana cigarette where she never remembered leaving it—right on their kitchen table! It resembled a piece of paper someone had been rolling, unrolling, and re-rolled.

The tip was burned but the joint was almost unsmoked! God, was this wicked strong shit or what! Hmm, should she smoke more, she wondered? Was it wrong? Or were all those people who said it was bad the wrong ones?

Some people needed medicines to get through their day, called "mood stabilizers" and prescribed by doctors. So why was grass any different if it worked for her? This was Win's happiest night ever—not just beginning a new decade of the 1970s, but discovering a new way of life as well! She joked to herself, Who knows, maybe I'll be one of those lucky ones that never comes down, hahah!

***

TUNING IN

Winnie wasn't one of the "lucky ones that never comes down," but instantly she started loving her life high on grass. She found what she'd been missing, and was off and running now! LSD was next—she never understood anything about God until taking it. In her quest to get higher and stay higher longer than was possible on grass, Acid Scott, the Acapulco Gold hippie met Win in the stinky dumpster alley behind her workplace, and gave her a chip no larger than a pin-head, of bright orange LSD. He called it Orange Sunshine, made by a famous San Francisco chemist named "Owsley," and the tiny pill appeared to throb with unknown powers like a granule-sized piece of the sun, scaring her to look at. It even seemed to sizzle in her sweaty palm and she worried it could fizz up and dissolve right into the thin frozen air.

"How strong is it?" she asked.

Scott tried to focus his big blue-green eyes on Win, and grinned. "I just took half a hit." He seemed almost childlike with innocence and openness, staring in awe at the squalid alley surroundings.

"Hmm… So, what is it like?"

Before replying, Scott gazed up the whole length of the alley. Next, he turned in the opposite direction to peer *down* the length of the alleyway. Finally, he placed a palm on the crud-encrusted dumpster as though conferring a blessing. "It is fan-*tastical!* Fan-tacular… I mean…ticularious."

Unlike before when he was just stoned, Scott's cherubic face was heavy serious, and his halo of flowers sat crooked. "You and God will be One," he pronounced, and hooked both of his index fingers together to simulate linkage. Then, Scott started studying his hand, absorbed in palm-reading himself or whatever by flexing the crease of his life-line from index finger down to the wrist.

Winnie didn't know what to think or do, but she had her doubts. Finally, Scott lifted his head, and stared straight into the middle distance, like cats do. "You see God everywhere."

"Oh, yeah…everywhere?" Win had a big skeptical grin, but her eyes narrowed along with Scott's as though trying to focus on a visual. "So, does God look like some Old White Guy on a throne, or a cloud, maybe… And a long beard?"

"Wrong!" Scott howled in laughter. "You talking about Jesus Claus!" he roared out before that dumpster altar of his.

"What about Jesus? You see Jesus, too?"

"Oh, Jesus, too!" he bellowed. "Now, Jesus—*Him*—that Guy! *He's got the real great stuff!*"

She couldn't tell if Scott referred to Jesus the man, Jesus the God, or a Hispanic. "So you think I need half a hit to see Jesus? Because I would really like to *see Jesus*. If I can."

"Na-ah," he scoffed. "You could even see Jesus without LSD. Jesus is the white guy. With a robe." In all seriousness, Scott nodded at the gutter running through the middle of the alley, so Win nodded, too. "Jesus is right next to Santa Claus on the throne! Jesus Claus for short!" Laughter erupted.

Soon, Scott was doubled over, and laughing hysterically for a minute straight, calling out, "Jesus Claus for short! Jolly

Jesus! Jesus is Claus! For short!" When he slowed down, his howls of glee would explode again, until Scott keeled over on the cratered pavement, delirious with joy about nothing! So, Winnie started shouting stupid stuff at him like, "Jesus in the the dumpster!" and "God is Claus!" But the poor guy couldn't talk; he was laughing so hard it resembled a seizure, painful, too. With only his wheezy little laughter audible, he writhed around the ground heaving in convulsions and thrashing like Pentecostals thrashed across the altar floor when God's Holy Spirit "enters" their body, or how Satan is depicted invading and taking possession of somebody in movies! He continued rolling on the pavement to control himself, but it was all too hilarious for Scott, he was gone! Maybe he had his "Oneness with God" and was already *in Heaven!* He sure acted happy enough! In fact he was way beyond ecstatic!

Wherever Scott's trip had taken him, nothing looked too bad there! Then, it had to be good, yes? Win ate the acid right away, and drove to the new Woodstock movie with her math club friend, Eve Foster, who began enjoying cocaine of late and wanted no part of the Orange Sunshine.

Win envisioned herself having that way-out Woodstock experience she missed in real life the previous summer. But, hours after eating the acid nothing spectacular happened. She felt almost the same, more antsy than usual, definitely buzzed but not much more. Except, the lyrics of Jefferson Airplane's "White Rabbit" started playing at strange times in her mind. "One pill makes you larger, and one pill makes you small… And if you go-o chasing rabbits, Tell 'em a hookah-smokin' caterpillar / Has given you the ca-all!"

During the Woodstock movie, whenever a song started, Eve took a sniff of coke from a handy little dispensing device she rigged up. It seemed coke was all she wanted these days, because she turned down the joints passed around the theater audience; she didn't even care about grass anymore, and Win almost asked her for a whiff of the stuff. But "White Rabbit" lyrics kept playing in her head, "When men on the chessboard get up and te-ell you where to go / And logic, and proportion have fallen sloppy dead…"

Except cocaine didn't appeal to Win. It was super-costly and people said the buzz lasted only minutes, so why bother, she wanted the opposite! Eve did offer her a toot to try, but she replied, "Aww. No, thanks, I'm looking forward to some Honduran buds before sleep." Then, more "White Rabbit" lyrics played, "And the Red Quee-en's o-off with her head! Re-member what the dormouse said, Keep Your HAI-ED!"

The moment Winnie unlocked the front door, her mother rolled off the couch—her head resembled an anvil, with one side of her hair completely flat where she was dozing on the armrest. "I wasn't asleep," she muttered with an eye opening. She looked like a zombie pretending not to be, then stumbled ahead with eyes still half-shut, and stopped to smell Win for alcohol. "You've been smoking cigarettes, but at least you're not drunk." She has *no* clue, thought Win! "Goo-o'd night!" she hiccupped. Her footsteps were heavy as she shuffled up to the master bedroom, and cracked open the door.

"I'm going to M.I.T., Mom, you don't have to wait up for me like I'm a child."

"Goodnight," she repeated with a downward finger jab.

"I can't sleep when you're out. You're like a stranger. Always out, new friends, late nights, I never feel safe anymore." Her mother made everything about her feelings; Win hated being a mere prop in her life, and after one last mistrustful look she withdrew into her dark bedroom, and Win withdrew to hers.

When she switched on the lights, there was a huge flash and the room seemed so much brighter than usual. The water pipe was filled with Honduran buds, waiting for Win to play her favorite record, Neil Young's *Everybody Knows This Is Nowhere,* with "Cinnamon Girl" and "Cowgirl In the Sand."

She lit the water pipe, and to her amazement she inhaled the entire bowl of grass in one single puff, without feeling a thing! Except the music didn't sound quite right, vocals were fading in and out. A turntable problem, she guessed... Maybe it was a loose wire, and she had a hilarious image of a loose wire zipping around her room like a crazy whipping snake; and followed by a horde of crazy whipping snakes! Then she realized that she could hardly hear the music. Neil Young's voice was like a babbling baby, and the instruments sounded thin and tinny like a child band playing "Cinnamon Girl" on ukuleles! Now what, a bad record too? Maybe the needle was tracking bad or jumping the groove. Time for a new record.

She played *Good Times, Bad Times* from Led Zeppelin with the Hindenburg exploding on the cover. This would say if the stereo was kaput! First, no sound came out. When she finally gave up and went to check the phonograph, the room exploded with thunderous deafening energy as the opening guitar chops struck, and echoed throughout! Win scrambled to turn down the volume, but she could not believe it was on the lowest setting! And her parents weren't screaming. Plus, the lights were throbbing in time to the music! God! No! She was hearing and seeing things which were impossible! It was Win, all inside her mind! These were real hallucinations!

Unlike the initial soaring euphoria she felt on grass, this was a paralyzing, terrifying panic, like that second before an inevitable car crash. Except each second was panic like that! This must be the real deal, what had been described to her as "peaking," or the heart of a full-on acid trip! But, this had to be a "bad trip," a "bum trip," that's what was happening!

A big bummer! Trapped here, paralyzed with fright and horror as the walls formed immense woofer-towers thumping out the heavy beats, and the bed danced with the bureau while the jealous window flew off the hinges to cut between them.

Just one thing was true—*nothing* was true! These were only visions, she kept assuring herself, nothing was actually going on, everything was the drug and the inventions of her imagination! But the hallucinations were every bit as real as Win sitting in her seat! This could be what insanity was like, all topsy-turvy, nothing but hearing and seeing and thinking horrifying things that were not happening! She pictured both of her parents bursting into the room, then going away, then returning and watching them yell at her but no sound coming from their mouths. Their faces changed shapes, and features were distorted. It was always them, though, no doubt of that! Things were not only topsy-turvy they were inside-out! But, unlike insanity, Win knew these visions had no validity, that was her sole anchor, one trusty lifeline connecting her back to life as she knew it—while she was drowning in this violent storm of bizarre images and maddening feelings of horror or paranoia. Another time, her parents busted into the bedroom yelling bloody murder but their lips didn't move! They were expressing outrage telepathically! Caricatures of people from her past pranced around; often their names escaped her.

But escaping the drug's immense power was impossible, it was in full control of her experience, and altered each split-second to anything but what was real. Even her hands passed through what she thought felt like solid objects. Finally, Win was surrendering herself to these all-consuming truths of the unreal, knowing only how she succeeded in taking that final flying leap over the edge where reality wasn't merely shifted like with grass, but almost everything she thought, felt, heard or saw is a delusion! Music whizzed around the bedroom, and she spotted several notes lurking in the shadows, forming and reforming into ocean waves with super-hunky surfer dancing guys on top, guitar licks zooming, whirring out tunes, drums and bass vibrating the walls and corners which all pumped in and out to the pulsing nuances.

Countless loose wires thrashed about like out-of-control fire hoses. And there was no relief when she closed her eyes. Instead, floods of intricate geometric patterns of every color and shape collided and melded in her mind's eye to generate endless reels of kaleidoscope images. Finally she was giving in to the only reality there was right at this very instant now, and the next instant, and the next. Trapped in here with only herself, only the music and experience of each supercharged second existed. Haunting refrains of "Dazed and Confused," and most terrifying of all, "Your Time Is Gonna Come!" kept echoing in the distance. Her rug resembled a magic weaving carpet on which she soared through her Milky Way bedroom, a ribbon beneath her feet of symmetrical patterns and colored arrays, all evolving differently like snowflakes.

Soon, she clicked into another gear, and became almost comfortable if not delighting in the experiences, but not until surrendering all of her will as well as her mind and the rest of herself to wave after wave of florid hallucinations; picturing the chemical faucets of her brain were thrown so wide open that every pathway and receptor was overflowing with neuro-transmitters, and her mind had to keep up with or stay ahead of the wild overstimulation by inventing a lot of unreal stuff to fill in her perceptions—presto, all these incredible visions! After ten tripping hours, which could not be imagined unless one went all the way to the other side themselves, she wanted more! The end of her trip was surprisingly enjoyable, relaxed and peaceful, like an infant exploring and learning from each remotely interesting new thing. Through her memories of the world, images and objects crossing her mind kaleidoscoped into reflections and fracture patterns. Refractions everywhere broke up, and rebuilt and reflected again in visual layers, with stunning insights and revelations about subatomic properties of matter and energy on the way! Comprehending the far out nature of the experience was tremendous fun. Ten solid hours of roller coasters, swirling day-glo collages, whip and splash rides, launch rides, free-fall rides, all extreme thrills at once might begin to describe it. Now that was some wicked strong shit or what!

This turned into a strange feeling of accomplishment, as

if she had survived a tremendous bad storm naked and alone in the night, which would have killed others. In truth, Win felt triumphant. She thought it spoke to some emerging personal power or unshakable faith that she had in herself. If nothing else, tonight's experience required unusual courage and self-control not to scream in terror about ten thousand times! Win gave herself extra credit, still unusual for her, and considered herself an excellent drug-taker! A natural. She might've been an ideal Druid or Delphic Oracle. Her self-esteem and grades improved as she discovered new interests with her expanded worldview. She was more social and popular now, too! Even Mr. van Beever looked at her different.

One of her next trips occurred with Eve Foster, and this was her friend's first exposure to hallucinogens. They ground up Magic Mushrooms, and were heading out to the Audobon Sanctuary behind Eve's house, where she bird-watched. But, somehow, they got stuck inside with Eve's parents and their whole family for a huge steak dinner! Worse still, on this trip Winnie began peaking almost immediately—during the first stinking bowl of fish chowder! She had all she could do not to repeat the accident of her mother's Persian rug; the steak was more repulsive, steaming in bloody animal fluids plus a putrid liver aftertaste. She thought she might never eat meat again. Eve saved the day by playing the Rolling Stones' live concert recording, *"Get Yer Ya-Ya's Out!"* Win was dancing alongside Eve's father to the song, "Carol" by Chuck Berry, his favorite tune from the '50s, as well as the name of Eve's mom. Then Eve's parents started jitterbugging together like teenagers, so the girls finally slipped out before dusk.

Laying in a cool meadow of tall grasses, Win felt herself floating away, being carried off the ground by gentle breezes lifting her up and up, then softly laying her back down, then lift again on a new breeze; sensing her outermost molecules merge with air layers, before releasing. Such sweet meadow grasses and wonderful flower scents combined for this ideal atmosphere in the sanctuary. With eyes closed, pulsing reels of visionary images unwound and morphed to the rushing of wind and birds chirping, as cartoon figures and synchronized ladybug armies paraded through her mind in kaleidoscoping patterns, flashing all their possible geometric configurations. Each color was the most vibrant she ever saw, the whitest of whites, much whiter than any whites should be. She saw how all things were—much more than ever seems at first like the whites; like physical reality is not only much deeper than ever appears, it is also much simpler and formed from the fewest elements in One unstoppable process of vital cosmic energy rendered in colors, geometrics, fractals galore!

In her blood and breath and in her bones, now she knew how she was constituted and shaped into this transient vessel for all the particles of her being, knowing that these particles of hers would go on for countless existences in the universe all are from. She was so thankful to know that, and *see* it in action too!

She rolled over on her belly and focused right on the tip of one tiny blade of grass. She visualized deep into the blade to see its lattice of veins with new electron-microscope eyes, examining the molecular cell structures by peering into each cell all the way down to their very atoms vibrating.

She pictured her electron-microscope eyes bugging out, registering her own astonishment with leaf cells channeling the light-absorbing chloroplasts, and forming constant green streams of chlorophyll which harness the sun's power before pumping it out through a complex network of veins. She sees millions of times magnification as these amazing leaf atoms achieve their miraculous conversion of photons into living energy. Cells divide and multiply right before her eyes with the plant growing in real time as fast as can be experienced, every split-second cells circulating from creation of our life force itself! From this—just from *this*—all life is fed! Then, seconds later, Win breathes in those same molecules she saw God create! What a sight! Actually experiencing or knowing Him—God—that teeny tiny Jesus Claus perched on a throne atop all these throbbing atoms she could see. God's unifying imprint was everywhere as in witnessing those very threads of His creation connected. God was always there—here—in the fibers and threads of the creation itself, but few ever *feel* or see God except through such spiritual experiences as this.

Now, God was visible in every tip of each little thing, in each hovering insect's tiny face. His was a vibration in every sound of birds and the wind, His blood rushing through the air as in flowing around all the knowns and unknowns of our existence; His Infinite processes melding into this Universal Oneness now and forever *with her—Winona Miller!*

She played with the hallucinations, and they were not so frightening. Reality was in the perception and here she could recognize how things flowed by or through all else into One.

Then, He showed up again—The Old White Guy—Jesus

Claus! Just another Happy Spirit with the wisest and kindest eyes, spreading such good stuff about. Winnie couldn't help think that if one wasn't seeing God in everything, one was not seeing God at all; call Him by any other name like Jesus Claus, and by those names He too shall come! For His was a face woven into the Eternal Mesh Of All Power.

In truth, though, her brain was just locked in hyperdrive. Drowning in neurochemicals, synapses firing at warp speeds saturated receptors, but her conscious mind met the demands of this supercharged processing power by tapping into more "enhanced perceptions" of what was always surrounding us, such as her extra-sensory experiences drawn from known or new stimuli and memory, which continuously soaked up the chemical tsunamis.

Finally, a ghoulish image of Winnie or her mom, with a flattened anvil-shaped head, horns and bloated face, named "THE BEAST," appeared in the mirror instead of Win's face.

A week later, when Winnie saw Eve again, it was a huge shock! She changed her limp turban hairstyle into a big red Afro!

"Wha-at! You don't dig my new Jew-fro?" Eve snarled; she was also changing into another person than the Eve Win had liked. But they never were close friends, Win still wasn't close to anybody. After their wild steak dinner and sanctuary trip, Eve made no effort to hang out so Win left her alone.

Eve went heavy into the cocaine, and also stopped going to school for some reason. She went nuts over the junk until threatened with expulsion; but soon that was a moot question when she gave the school's headmaster a good shove before dropping off the radar, and never did go to Harvard after all. Senior slumps were one thing, but Eve dive-bombed into that dummy dust. A year later, Win saw on the news how Eve got caught smuggling cocaine at the airport, then burned through an $800,000 trust fund over-indulging her cocaine habit until suffering a fatal coronary. It was not possible to comprehend how or why such a super-smart girl could let that happen, so she decided never to do cocaine. Everyone she knew who did landed in bad trouble, most sooner rather than later. Perhaps her grades weren't as good as Eve's, but she had the sense to steer clear of coke or anyone tooting that stuff.

It was tough to learn about Eve's tragedy since Win was so content with the happiness and fun afforded by her magic herbs. If life itself did not naturally provide what helped her feel as normal or as well as others but the herbs did, then she deserved it! Why wouldn't Winnie deserve to feel as good as others could feel without a medicine?

She never wanted to lose her new sense of wonderment for a second. She considered drugs to be just another path for turning people into the spiritual beings they were meant to be anyway, with no trappings of civilization. Different tools did exist, it was true, but this is what she liked, understanding the natural and fundamental state of the universe had nothing to do with control, or even substance for that matter. Instead, it was a profound experience of unification for her, immersion into an eternal hum of background energy, the cosmic deep-field of sublime sensation, permeating and inspiring our own conscious dreamworld with a fascination for the miraculous. Just think if we lived like that! Win wanted to live like that!

DROPPING OFF

For 20 years Winnie loved living her life like that, until a friend from work that she never thought would do cocaine, broke some out at a party with a bunch of other cool people, and when everybody looked to be having an especially good time, she was offered a small amount.

"I've never done it," Win replied. "Just seen lots of good people go down the drain on that stuff."

"Oh, no! This is super good, real pure." Her friend's face shined with genuine wamth. She echoed Eve Foster's claim 20 years ago about grass being "super" good and was so true for Win. Despite all the trouble that Eve and others got into, for some reason she considered giving "blow" a try…to see.

"No. I'm not sure. I mean, I kind of would like to."

"Gotta try 'toots' once in your life!" scoffed her friend. "Go on! Such a cool girl," she encouraged further, implying it was hard to believe, or time for change. Then, she clicked a cheek and grinned. "It doesn't hurt, I promise!" Laughing.

"Well… Maybe… Just to see what the fuss is. Because I know you wouldn't want me to do anything *bad* for me."

Win went ahead and sniffed a big fluffy rail, then forgot it and had a nice time. The next month, at another party, she also did a few rails. Then she snorted more and at the end of the night bought a small quantity. Winnie didn't believe she could make the same mistakes as the others had. That's how she began. With plenty of savings, common sense and salary increasing all the time, she never imagined stealing or dying like those she knew of who crashed and burned on the stuff. Win was confident that she could handle it in small amounts, and made some room for it in her life.

But in a short time she formed a deep secret relationship with coke, telling herself and others, "I feel nice, it helps me cope with my insecurities so I don't feel bad, or hate myself for making mistakes. I still feel OK when I screw up which is new for me, and healthier since I'm such a lazy perfectionist. In a weird way, it almost seems to care about me and how I feel more than the actual me! It understands my weaknesses, my fears and what I need like no one else can, and keeps me from criticizing myself too much regardless of who is trying convince me I'm bad, or wrong. My 'toots' are more like my friends without judgments—they only want to be loved, and wanted in return, like me!"

For Winnie, cocaine was a substance that unleashed the devil lurking inside everybody, the lying, cheating, stealing, betraying devil; the one who descends into evermore serious personal and financial trouble which is never their fault; and finally the one who stops eating, sleeping, showering or even brushing their teeth.

Long story short, within eight months Winnie was fired, lost her assets, good name, and developed a condition called delusional parasitosis, commonly called "coke bugs," where she became obsessed about insects constantly crawling under her skin. She reached to the brink of death numerous times from seizures, accidents and other self-destructive mayhem, before recognizing that the life she had now resembled little more than hitting a bar as much as possible for coke—to the exclusion of all else—just another doomed rat in a Skinner Box; until she was one more…dead thing.

When stabbing bolts of pain start knifing down her neck and spread around like needles instead of blood are shooting through her veins, and she wakes up on the ground days after her last memory with flesh peeled away to dig out the "coke bugs," it spelled the end of *that!*

As if defeated after a long heroic struggle, she mourned for her regretful self, "This was your last *last* chance. Next time, we don't wake up. You won't, almost no chance." But Win knew it was over when she was happier about not living with the coke bugs again, than she was about living itself.

She looked back only to acknowledge how nothing was fun for such a long time, not since she began when it jumped over from a one-time gratification thing, straight into a thing of wanton indulgence for its own never-to-be-satisfied sake. Nor would it be fun to do again; knowing the certain end for her, she couldn't enjoy it, or escape anymore either. This had no other way to end except for enough. Or dead.

***

As close as she was to losing her life, she may have just one second chance to make the best of that reprieve. Winnie became thankful and happy again, knowing she could go on being happier still, and have anything else she wanted in life, except if she did cocaine again. Not that she didn't know this intellectually, now it exploded like a bomb in her face that it wasn't enough; she also had to accept—and forever keep—a sacred pact with the universe through which she travelled. A far more potent conviction and connection to her Source than intellect beckoned, coming by way of a covenant, a promise that she sensed was being extended to her, and also carried favorable terms. So, Win pledged her soul—she would keep free of her great demonic temptation, coke, and let the rest of her life bear its rightful fruits, probably beyond any dreams. Yet, the core of her promise or "pact with the universe" was an ultimatum, and even a sacred bargain like hers was often resented if unconsciously. She was not so resentful about her own strict terms, though; she could envision surrendering her worst possible devil-self and accommodating life around the plain certainty of the pact.

Most had a similar tragic flaw, a weakness so irresistible yet disagreeable with their truest spirit, its existence cancels out their own and guarantees undoing. Yet, if one were able to overcome that vulnerability, it can be a reliable rudder or fulcrum from which to leverage a fulfilling life, where all the good they were and still would be, may flourish, by virtue of not giving in to their one tragic temptation.

Just that condition, the crux, the promise to herself and the universe, zero coke. Coke was so corrosive it is one drug that gives drugs a bad name. Worse still, cocaine was a fatal match to Win's unique set of vulnerabilities and thus was a guarantee of never reaching her dreams or much else in life. With such vulnerabilities, there were no gray areas for Win. Her weakness was far too strong to risk it sinking its teeth in her again. Using coke again equated to choosing death above anything; not doing it held the door open for all the blessings to come her way that a long great life would afford. And she didn't even have to give up grass! *WhattaDeal!* This wisdom was her simple sauce for enduring happiness—plus whatever was legal and felt good that wasn't coke!

Happiness was a simple Yes-No thing, clear as anyone's "road to happiness" could be! Yet, given such a clear logical choice between happiness or death, it was nearly impossible to comprehend how strong her weakness remained! Lurking in the weeds was always the slimmest chance of succumbing to a temptation—whether that chance be a fraction of 1% or not, it came with dreadful sensations she never would shake off, and were terrifying in themselves. Yet, the cruelest irony was the only sure way of crushing them was nose-diving into another pile of dummy dust, and escape once and forever. A crux to bear for life.

At least for the time being Win's road of excess did lead her to the Palace of Wisdom, per Blake's quote. How—or if it stayed this way through life—would be a conscious choice to let pass by any time she got more urges or notions about trashing that sacred covenant that she kept with her Source, and do one dumb thing.

Eve must have faced a lot of the same struggles with her own temptations, and fall from grace. Though Eve may have been granted the most favorable covenant imaginable in this universe, she just would not trust her Source enough to help her ditch that worst willful version of herself, or surrender to Its truth.

Instead, she just surrendered to Its truth.

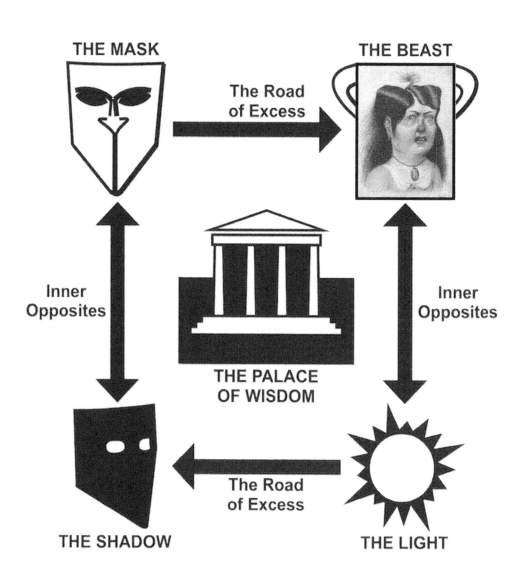

Masks of Wisdom

DIVING FOR DOPE
(Drive In the Rear)

Stressed-out Earl tries to trade unwanted drugs for scuba diving gear, resulting in ridiculous problems.

The entrance to Hector's apartment complex was a few hundred feet away, but Earl was so nervous trying to be on time, he took a right where he should've gone left, got lost in a dark construction zone, then went through the same railroad crossing three times before almost killing a homeless shopping-cart pusher on the tracks. He had the directions on his phone, left in plenty of time and yelled at himself, "Goes to show, Earl, the stupidest crap *always* screws *you* up!"

Puffy-faced Hector met him at the nearest corner with a big scowl, and led Earl to his Evergreen Terrace complex. A sign in front said, "Entrance In The Rear."

Earl tried to explain, "None of these one-ways or dead ends are marked in my GPS!" Then he got angry with Hector for being angry at him!

Hector had his wife's scuba equipment and Earl brought a bag of tranquilizers they were going to bargain over. Earl was supposed to take the pills when he felt like he "needed" them, which was almost never. But, thinking they could come in handy someday, he filled the prescription each month so at this point he had a big jarfull, and was confident about his chances of getting like-new diving gear in return!

They were alone right now, but Hector's wife would be arriving later from her church charity work. She had recently converted to a fundamentalist Christian sect and forsaken "all things of the world," said Hector, pushing aside schematics he was examining so Earl could sit. "My wife, though, she is a true intellectual. Married 15 years now." He pointed upward as in being blessed. "Thirteen years older than me, too."

Hector himself was older than Earl, a burly 45-year old master electrician who seemed responsible and noble to the hilt like his namesake in *The Iliad,* but would not go through his company's health plan to get a legal drug.

Each had a beer, and Earl got curious about the company Hector worked for, which was completely anti-drug, legal or not. "The owners are the same about abortion," he said. "No abortions. Not even if the woman was raped. Or the baby will be born a cripple."

Earl thought to himself, That is extreme righteousness! "Let me guess," he remarked, "Anti-gay marriage, too?"

"Oh, bro!" He plopped his big forearms on the tabletop in front of Earl. "Me! I know." He gestured at himself. "Other workers, my compadres, had prescribed tranguilizers and the bosses found out through the HMO. My friends all got extra work, they got the worst jobs, until they left. No kidding. My union is weak in this state, and I'm a foreman now, I got my Journeyman's License to protect. We can't let no one know I got tranquilizers."

For selfish reasons Earl was not going to argue with him although he did seem too concerned. "Once it's on the record, they got you for life, dude." Hector emphasized by waving an arm back and forth in a wipe-out motion. There were various dramatic gestures such as long deep breaths, and using both hands to rake back his mane of shoulder-length black hair.

Earl disliked being addressed as "dude" or "bro" which Hector also called him, but he overlooked it to avoid possible antagonism. His eyes were dead set on scoring the equipment cheap so he didn't mention privacy laws. In fact, he reinforced Hector's paranoia. "Yes, you're right, insurance people suck, they don't respect anybody's reputation, or job. They always share sensitive information with companies, it's no secret, so greedy employers take advantage if they can."

A bird squawked from the other room. "Right...right, so yeah, you know what I'm sayin' there, bro."

"I've heard lots of horror stories, Hector. Sure, you have to look out," he poured it on. "I get you, dude."

Not that Earl cared if the company was run by righteous zealots, but there may be cause for concern; it didn't matter, anyway; this was *only* about scuba gear! Hector didn't trust him, though, insisting he come alone while limiting what he knew in case Earl would try to harm him somehow, not even caring about what the true value of the dive equipment was. He also would not name his company—as if Earl could be a DEA agent! However, Hector invites him right into his living room and he couldn't see how big a contradiction that was!

Earl almost laughed when Hector told him, "See, dude, my wife, she thinks I'm being paranoid."

"Na-aw… Really?" Earl decided to get down to business and began explaining to this guy, "So, Hector, here's the deal, each month I tell a doctor, I say, 'Doctor, sir, I feel this or that way,' and he gives me these pills. But I never take them—"

"I'm wanting to save some money too, bro," interrupted Hector. As a foreman, he must unconsciously address others that bro-way. "This ain't no drug deal, you understand. This is a discount diving deal." He jabbed his finger on the table.

"Yeah, I want it that way, too. Just a good fair deal." Earl pulled out his baggie with 250 tranquilizers. One pill would seriously phase a normal person but was still a ridiculous low price for the gear. On the street, those pills might be worth a couple hundred dollars, but at the pharmacy it was $15, and Earl's HMO pays 80% of that! So, he was shooting to score this gear for $3 out-of-pocket! Just a good deal! Sure, dude!

Earl handled his problems just fine without pills, even irritations such as being called "bro," or "dude," or fingernail clippings on the table like here. As much as anyone, he hated his job and his living situation, which had nothing to do with taking or not taking his pills. They made him dumb or sleepy, anyway. For Earl, there was no comparison to the wonderful relaxing feelings of diving. What a tremendous combination of sensations, dreamy, excited, calming all at the same time! Fascinating and death-defying, too. He loved it! One dive in the morning and he felt terrific all day, happy, relaxed, and a bit high! What more is there to have or to feel, he wondered!

He daydreamed about diving, about those super gliding sensations, like flying through everything but better because of the weightlessness, and the risk, the danger, right there on the edge but still alert, with the spectacular sights only a few feet underwater, and ten times more a hundred feet below it. Who needed drugs, or anything else! Diving had everything, including the excitement of exploration and discovery at any turn, life and death challenges all the time, not to mention the beauty and thrills of going to another world for real, it's the ultimate organic experience! Nothing beats those all-natural flows of adrenaline combining with Raptures of the Deep, to fine-tune his own satisfaction his own way! Earl concluded it was just another addiction, more perilous than drugs in many ways. And legal! He wanted to try mountain climbing, too.

"Give me one of those pills to try," Hector demanded.

Earl obliged, and Hector gulped it with another swig of beer. "Don't drink alcohol when you take these," he warned.

"Na-ah, one beer… You sound like my wife now." Even the way he pulled his hair back, and plopped his big arms on the table was dramatic. Earl wondered, Why is he doing that? So, he decided Hector's mannerisms were bugging him a lot.

The insistent bird screeched from the bedroom, and Earl wanted to check it out. Birds usually took to him right away, but this one, a green and gray macaw with a can-opener for a beak, went berserk when Earl approached the cage.

"Hey, back off, bro. Samantha guards that cage with her life. First, the perch," he instructed. Hector opened the door, and inserted a stick which the bird perched on. But, when he transferred the bird to Earl's arm, she was none too pleased, and Earl had to keep calm as Samantha tested her tender new perch by leisurely chewing on a chunk of his meaty forearm with the spike beak.

The instant before anguished Earl was about to whip her off his arm, Hector admonished the bird, "You know better than that!" He tapped her on top of the flourishing head-crest and returned her to the cage. "Hey, other people, she just goes right onto them. I'm surprised she did that to you." He made a quizzical look, focusing his eyes on Earl while he winced in pain. "Hey, you sure you're not a DEA agent there, bro?" He did not expect a real answer though.

Earl felt lightheaded from the throbbing ache, massaging his fleshy inner forearm where two imprints of the upper and lower beak were embedded, with a trickle of blood flowing. "Ga-wd, that frikkin' hurt…"

"OK!" declared Hector. "I'm feeling good on what you gave me. Let's deal." Happy Hector now spread out the dive gear in the living room. Seeing all the stuff in new condition bumped up Earl's mood. The 120 cubic foot tank was filled and had recent test markings stamped in the steel. The gauges and dive computer had big displays, the buoyancy jacket was never used, and it also included a mask he could talk through and insert prescription lenses. This was a dream.

Hector wanted $650 for everything. And Earl hesitated. He agonized. But why wouldn't he take advantage of it? He wasn't pulling the trigger—yes, he was squeezing the trigger, Hector was right in his sights, but the finger felt frozen half-way through! Hector changed his expression and his position in the seat. Maybe Earl waited too long! Then, Hector blurted out, "Five-hundred! That's it. Botton line."

They agreed on $450 for the gear but best of all, Hector took the whole bag of pills in lieu of any cash! Simple deal!

Earl didn't realize how important the drugs were to Hector. A fair price for the gear was irrelevant. On the other hand, Earl just wanted something for the pills, a couple hundred bucks or maybe a little more. But he got much more from Hector! This was close to stealing! Almost too good to be true. Yet, it was!

Who wouldn't do this deal even if they didn't care about diving? It was a can't-miss proposition! Although, it did feel something like a drug deal. And stealing! But, who's kidding whom? It was illegal, both were risking a lot, both gambling on their own "fixes."

"I'm going to take another one now," Hector announced and took a second pill. Earl was about to say something again but decided not to distract himself from assembling his stuff, and leaving fast. "My wife, Dee, I don't think you know, bro, she's 13 years older than I am. A true intellectual. Reads like a demon, a Book-a-Day for her—forget about a Book-of-the-Month Club—she's one a day. Now she's given all that up." He twisted open another beer. "She's not 'in the world' any more. Being 'in the world,' it's everything that's not directly *'for God.'* Like the diving…beer…reading. She only reads church literature now. Plus, her Bible." Hector emphasized by dramatically pulling back his thick mane. "Lover, mother, wife, intellectual, my best friend." With both hands he raked back the hair again to maximize the effect. Inebriation? Earl was getting so annoyed by these mannerisms of his.

Earl replied, "That's great, Hector." All he could think of was a graceful way to get out. "That's so difficult to find," he added, as his brain went blank. "Especially if somebody changes so quick. Like Dee." Earl fumbled with the weights and bulky equipment, his tank, the hoses, etc., while Hector leaned back, and rambled away.

"Well, her father died last year…she needed something new, another outlet to deal with it, bro. So, I just let her go." These were noble sentiments, but he also seemed quite high, while disclosing personal details about Dee and her only son by a previous marriage, Adam, who had turned 19 and was on his third job this year. Hector showed pictures of his wife and the boy. Dee looked 10 years younger than Hector said, and the boy was a giant, at least 6' 7" and as much as 300 pounds. "He's the Weenie," joked Hector. "That's what I call him."

Then, the phone rang. It was the "Weenie." Hector spoke to him with a big smile, "What do you want? More money?" Then a pause. "You know where your mother is, she is where she wants you to go—to the church." Another pause. "Well, you know what they sayin, bro, you gotta get away from that bunch, that's bad news," he told the Weenie.

Earl was nervous about further delays, and the gear was assembled now so they could carry it down to the car in one trip. After getting off the phone, Hector helped put everything at the door where he paused to show Earl more Weenie-Mom pictures, saying, "See, the Weenie's real father works around the world. He's a pro diver, too, repairs ships, oil rigs, makes ridiculous *great* money. But, I've been the kid's real father for 15 years. I'm the one he goes camping with, driving, and biking with. The one his friends like to be with, too, bro."

"Is he in a gang, or something?" Earl didn't care but he thought some comment should be made.

"Yeah, sort of a gang. Yeah." He eyeballed Earl but in an

almost friendly way now. "Kind of a gang. Aw, hell, let's just take another of these." Hector went to pop another pill when Earl stopped him.

"Take it easy, Hector. Those are stronger than you think. And don't drink." He took the new beer out of Hector's hand and poured it down the drain.

Instead of arguing, Hector plunked his hefty body back down at the kitchen table. "Oh, yeah, 'Don't drink anymore, Hector, Don't drink anymore.' My wife only says it a couple times a night, but *you*—you're three times in a half hour!"

Earl couldn't help thinking there was more to this whole thing. Hector would spend hundreds more to get tranquilizers this way, plus the dive equipment? It was a steep price rather than going to a doctor and getting it legally for just $3! Made no sense, "But, hey, whatever, bro!" Earl ridiculed the guy's voice in his head. Their deal was done and Earl was about to open the front door when a key turned in the lock outside.

Hector scrambled up and tossed the bag of tranquilizers into the trash with empty beers on top. The urgency surprised and worried Earl. "I don't want my wife thinking that we're drinking too much," he spoke softly. "Hello! Who's there?" he raised his voice. "Who is it?"

"Hector, it's me, Adam. What is going on in there?" the son called through the door. "Take the chain off the door."

"The Weenie…" Hector whispered.

"The Weenie…" Earl repeated. What now?

"The Mom's not far behind, either, dude. They're home real early."

"Is there something to worry about?"

"No. Don't worry, you want the equipment. We have this understanding, you know." Concern was written all over his creased and puffy face.

I'd be fine if I was out 5 minutes earlier! Earl yelled at himself. Maybe. Maybe not, too. Even when I do everything right, the shit still screws up! he berates himself. But, didn't I do whatever possible! Didn't I? he wondered.

"Mom's right here, Hector!" Weenie's big voice boomed through the crack in the door as Hector unhooked the chain.

The door swung inward. Hector's wife breezed in first, a glowing radiance on her pretty round face, exuding liveliness especially for 58, and accompanied by Adam who ambled in behind her like a freakish overgrown teenager. Both seemed surprised that anyone was with Hector.

"I'm Dee," she introduced herself.

"Hello," Earl greeted them, and shook her hand. "Hector and I were just making a deal for diving gear. And, you must be Adam." Earl extended his to shake, but Adam's was limp, and given his size it caused a strange creepy feeling. He also never bothered to look Earl's way and climbed over the back of the couch, plopping hard on the seat and snatching up the first thing to read.

"As far as I'm concerned, you can have it all," said Dee. "Just leave your cash on the table." She marched away to her bedroom while Hector and Earl glanced at each other. Hector looked miffed, and made a Wait-and-See hand gesture before charging into the bedroom after his wife, and closed the door.

"So, you want to steal the dive gear?" Adam sneered at Earl. Adam wore an oversized orange top with ACTIVE ZX logo, which also matched his orange half-pants and high-top sneakers. "I wanted the gear but my Mom's boyfriend there, Hector, he wants to trade it for pills, he even tried to get me to help! No way. Screw him. I told my Mom, and that's why she wants to see cash."

Earl's heart skipped some beats, then it sank. He hated himself for fumbling with the equipment, and chatting. "So, did you meet your Mom at church?" he changed the subject.

"How did you know about that?" He sounded all nasty and confrontational. "Nothing. When you called, Hector said where she was. Then, he showed me your pictures." Voices were audible from the bedroom, punctuated by bird squawks. "So, were you thinking of going to church with your mom?"

"I don't know nothin' *Dood!*" he replied with contempt. His big round face was contracted uglily to reflect his mood, and Earl thought of calling him "Weenie," to watch him get super angry, and perhaps he would attack. Lawsuit material! Ha-hah. Earl laughed to himself. That was a stupid thought.

The bedroom door flew open, and Dee charged out with the frightening bird on her shoulder. Hector followed with a defeated look, like a sulking boy.

Earl spoke up, "I apologize, Dee. Is something wrong?" This was such a terrific deal but the Weenie wanted the stuff too, and probably some pills. Dee just wanted cash, probably to pay bills, give to the church and control her husband. Pills definitely weren't part of any deals for her, though! "Perhaps I should let you figure out what you want to do?" suggested Earl. Another problem was the pills went in the trash beneath the beers, and he couldn't leave without those. Nor could he get them back without screwing things up worse for Hector.

Dee questioned Earl, "How much cash do you bring?"

"A hundred dollars." Earl told the truth.

She studied Hector's dark puffy face, then decided. "OK. Give it to me," she said. "You can have the gear for $100."

Earl's mouth dropped open, and he was so surprised that again he did not agree right away.

"No! No!" Both Hector and the Weenie protested.

"I thought…but…my birthday," Weenie argued his part as an entitled son. He was a perfect Baby Huey type, doughy white face with a thick, high-and-tight buzz cut.

But, what about the pills, Earl wondered? Hector would keep them. OK, he reasoned, so the gear cost 100 bucks and the pills, which cost him next to nothing and he would not use anyway, so it was still fine! Now he had to interrupt.

"It's all my stuff," Dee claimed, putting her hands up to Adam and Hector. "Don't argue with me! And give this man back his drugs if you have any, Hector," she added. "Get that stuff out of here, you don't need that."

It was so low for the gear that Earl felt a need to confirm. "Are you sure?" he tried to sound cautious while not granting that the regulator alone was worth over twice the amount.

The Weenie stomped big circles around everyone, beside himself with resentment and frustration. Hector tried to pull his wife back, so Earl interrupted them again. "Um, OK, Dee, I agree… It's a deal… OK?"

But, at that moment Dee pulled further away from him to argue with Hector. The Weenie re-joined their argument, his big baby-face contracted in disgust.

What the hell was Earl thinking? He didn't have any clue. Sometimes he couldn't think straight. What did he care about Hector not having his pills or Adam getting nothing, or Dee fighting with either one about the gear, or God or whatnot? Pick up all the gear like it's yours for $100! Earl screamed at himself. It's yours! She already said so! Or figure out how to get your pills back and get out now! Get out of here!

They continued their heated conferencing. The fearsome bird was quiet, though. "I'll do it, yes," Earl tried to interrupt their argument again. "Dee… Umm."

Then, she snapped at Earl, "Wait! It's No Deal yet!" So, everyone stopped arguing, and glared at Earl. That was that. They kept conferring. He was pissed at himself for hesitating those split seconds. I am a mess! he punished himself. Maybe I did need some drug after all. Like Hector. Maybe I'd make better decisions by thinking through things more with meds.

Earl approached them inch by inch, another bad decision when the macaw stunned everybody by flying at his head!

Earl ducked away! But she landed on his upper sleeve as he cringed. She didn't dig her claws into him, though. Instead everyone held their breath to watch Samantha's intentions in climbing up on Earl's shoulder. But, she perched right there, and remained quiet, to their surprise and amusement.

"E-hh. She does like you, after all," said Hector. "See?" he added in Dee and Adam's direction. "This guy, he's OK."

The bird nibbled Earl's ear lobe, who was terrified with that ice pick of a beak probing the area. Still, he was feeling Samantha's gentle breathing in two tiny puffs of air from her nostrils into his ear. Even Weenie looked less hostile. In that multi-colored suit of yellows, orange, with black pockets and trim, the Weenie didn't seem a violent guy as much as trying to fit in somewhere and somehow, along a continuum of the least resistance.

"No, no!" Hector raised his own voice. "I buy the things for you, Dee-Dee, I can say what happens, too. No?

"No! You know that it isn't working like that, Hector!" Dee lapsed into the slang. "No, no. What you buy for me and give to me is mine!"

One by one, Hector then Adam peeled away from Dee, who addressed Earl directly again. "Tell me the real deal you and Hector make up. Or else you not be getting the stuff for cheap!" She amused herself by the power she wielded over the men. So Earl decided to play ball with her all the way.

The bird's sharpened tusk nibbling on the earlobe was more insistent, and he feared at any moment she may test the puncture-resistant qualities of his chewable ear cartilage.

"Samantha, stop that!" Dee scolded, eyeballing the bird, who immediately squawked an ear-splitting complaint right into his ear canal, then backed away, raising and lowering her gorgeous frightening head. But, soon she started tugging and pulling on the seams of his shirt. "So, what was your deal?" Dee smiled back at Earl. "Cash? And some pills?"

"There was nothing finalized," Earl lied. But why would he? He was such an idiot, maybe she *gives* him everything if he only tells her the truth! Dee didn't care about the gear or money, all she wanted was truth. And power over her men.

"How much cash?" she demanded.

Earl looked at Hector, and admitted, "A little more than

a hundred." Earl breathed hard.

"What is it with *all* you guys—never a straight answer! Well, here's my deal—we putting everything on hold." Then, she studied Earl. "Are you a doctor that prescribe pills, so you promise Hector you do it for the gear? Like that?"

"No. I know a doctor… He might prescribe a medicine. If you say the right thing."

"But, Hector, why you don't just go to the doctor then if you want this medicine?" she argued.

"You know, the HMO, Dee-Dee. My promotion…what happened with Jesus. You know…" he said with a pleading gesture, then glanced at Earl, too.

"Honestly, Hector, you are getting to be too much," she argued. "Maybe it's not even medicine you need. Maybe just counseling. Or a vacation!"

"A-achh!" scoffed Hector. "A vacation—with three new towers going up!" He sat back down at the cramped kitchen table, frowning at Earl and all that nice equipment piled up to go. Regretfully, Hector shook his head in defeat. "Sorry, dude, it's maybe no deal tonight. Looking like."

"Oh… Not a problem, dude," Earl tried not to sound too miffed or disappointed. "Call me later."

"We'll be in touch…" promised Hector with an upward eyebrow movement.

Dee went to remove Samantha from Earl's shoulder like reclaiming property. But, to everyone's surprise the bird was resting there, balanced on one leg, and made small sounds of protest at the interruption.

All said quick Goodbyes and Earl left empty-handed, so

upset he didn't realize until reaching the car that he forgot his tranquilizers *again!* He hurried to the door and hit the buzzer. Dee answered. "Dee, I might have left something up in your apartment."

In the background, he heard her asking Hector whether he found anything, and Hector replying, No, that he didn't.

Earl gave up. Then, he suddenly got angry again. Unless he told Dee about the pills Hector would keep those, too! He was so conflicted about fighting to get them, but what did he care if Hector got in any more trouble with Dee, going so far as to consider dropping an anonymous "Crime Stoppers" tip at his job to drug test Hector, or something as despicable.

Then, he realized he did not know the company's name, so Hector was a little smarter or luckier than Earl gave him credit for, in some way at least.

"Oh, wait a second, Earl!" Dee's voice came back over the intercom. "Hector's coming down. You left your keys!"

Earl gripped his pockets. "Oh… U-huh, yes. My keys." He forgot his keys, too! He was such a goddamn mess! Not even a "hot mess," just a *sad* mess, who could not get almost anything to go right! He probably did need tranquilizers. Or, something!

Hector showed with his keys, and totally surprised Earl with the pills, too, making him thankful at least for the safe return of his whole $3 worth of pills!

"Sorry, again, bro," he told Earl. "I took those, and didn't like them. I don't think those are the ones for me. My wife's usually right. I should see a doctor first. This is too much like a drug deal."

"Maybe you're right," he conceded. It was disappointing, losing a chance to get rid of the tranquilizers in exchange for something that really was fun. Perhaps Earl could pay cash for the gear and still get a good deal though! "What are you going to do with the gear?" he inquired.

"I think she may want to give it to the Weenie, it's better for us, doing things in the family, you know? I got my family, that is Number One. Gotta listen to that lady, you know. Me and the Weenie, we going out diving this weekend. He wants to start a diving class, become an instructor… He says that now. So, you know, we probably gonna give it a chance. Maybe." He motioned with his head as if saying, We hope for the best.

"Maybeee…" Earl agreed with similar optimism. "The Weenie…" he repeated, nodding for no apparent reason.

"The Weenie, yeah, that's right."

Earl added, "Can't think of a better story for you or your wife—Weenie in business, finds God! Makes people proud!"

"Yeh, man," Hector plays along. "Like that…yeah, bro."

"So, put in a good word for me with the Ween, will ya!" Both laughed.

"The Weenie don't like you. The bird did not like you. I didn't like you," he said with a friendly grin. "Man you sure turned that all around."

"Even the bird likes me now!"

"Na-ah, you respected my wife, bro. Weenie liked that."

"One of these days let's go on a dive together, you, me, and maybe the Weenie!"

"Maybe, man. Maybe," he reflected on it with a glimmer of possibility.

Adam appeared while they were joking, and didn't seem to think their Weenie bantering was funny.

"Oh, hello, Adam," Earl greeted him. "Good luck on that new diving venture."

He immediately got into Earl's face. "Don't 'Adam' me, dude. You were calling me 'Weenie.' *Don't ever* do that!" He jabbed his forefinger into Earl's soft middle-chest, digging it into the heart area while Earl gave ground. "Only Hector can call me that. I still hate it!" Earl's only thought was to shove back hard. But, again, a little voice inside said, Do not do it!

Weenie turned away, as Earl carefully reconsidered any reaction. "I was wishing you the best luck, Adam, that's all."

"I know! I know!" he shot back, and suddenly he started pacing around in circles, fast, ever-so-stylish in those black high-tops, orange shirt and matching half-pants, with the big black pockets and trim. Half Earl's age, but totally dominates him when he wants to. Adam mumbled while he paced, and chastised himself with, "Cool that shit out, Ween," and, "He is a guest," and, "Don't act up now." Adam appeared to regret climbing all over Earl, but with somebody else that results in a serious bad beat-down.

An old Black guy showed up beside them, pushing all his worldly possessions in a shopping cart with one crazy wheel spinning, and he asked them for a quarter. He looked like the same bum Earl almost hit on the tracks earlier. Even six feet apart he smelled like a soiled butt crack. Earl was suspicious of such a modest request and declined, noting the dirty man's eyes—both whites were as big as saucers, clear and sparkled with true aliveness for such a down and out bum. Weenie and

Hector reached in their pockets.

"Why t'ank you, my brothers," said the derelict, and also thanked Earl, making him feel more guilty for his cheapness.

Hector was moving well for someone ripped on beer and tranquilizers. Maybe it hits him later! Earl stared at Weenie for a few seconds and, feeling generous, showed him the pill bag. "You want some of these?"

Adam's face opened wide like a door swinging open to a breathtaking view. "Yeah." He took the bag, and scooped out a handful.

"You want more, go ahead."

"Nah," Hector stepped in. "That's enough." He made Earl take back the rest of the bag. "Oh, hell," Hector reconsidered, taking another big handful for himself. "Thanks, bro."

Hector and the Weenie laughed mischievously, bumping fists in celebration as a few pills dropped on the pavement.

"No problem." Earl had four year's worth at home, and would keep the rest of this bag, too, bent on getting a meager value from them somehow.

Then, he regretted doing this in an open parking lot with many apartments looking down on them. He wasn't thinking again! He was constantly rubbing his arm from the bird bite, and feeling an increasingly warm tingle as if an inflammatory process were also taking hold.

"That's nothing," Hector remarked. "That's a love bite. If she was really wanting to hurt you, she has bone-crushing power." He laughed at Earl again, along with the Weenie.

Once inside the car, Earl checked his newest tranquilizer prescription, and noted his own hand trembling. On that note

Earl left Hector's apartment complex, and right away caught himself driving 60 in a 30 MPH zone, with his jaw clenched so tight that his teeth were grinding.

Earl let up on the gas, took in a deep breath and gasped, realizing that he crushed the prescription slip while trying to relax the other parts of himself! Then, he almost hits another homeless guy crossing the tracks in front of him! Goddamn! "What is it with all the frikkin' homeless!" He pounds both fists on the steering wheel until they are bruised, and throb.

"God, I should try taking a couple pills," he thought, and gobbled two as prescribed, which almost immediately made him feel better. To Earl, it meant that even if he was conning the doctor or the doctor prescribed them because of what he saw or what Earl said, there was a problem somewhere. So it was good that he didn't get his head pounded down his throat by the Weenie over nothing, perhaps his best move all night!

After taking the medicine everything else seemed to flow more smoothly, from the car shifting its gears to the scenery, to a pleasant new series of thoughts. It was a shame how the evening worked out. Although a few hundred bucks worth of equipment wasn't worth his happiness as a person.

Unfortunately, the long swooping shadow of a police car closed the distance behind him, and appeared to be following. Normally he would get super nervous, but not this night. He had some prescribed medicines in the car, and hadn't broken any laws. The cop drove up beside him at the next light with full antennae prickling up, and seemed to be trying to get his attention with a long look over, and a little revving.

Earl turned up his music and kept staring straight ahead.

Unless the cop pulled him over for breaking a law, there was no obligation to acknowledge him, so Earl did not. But, after tailing him for miles, the cop fired up his array of lights and did stop him.

"License and Registration," he barked. This trooper was not an imposing figure, short, skinny, and bald as a poop. His diarrhea-brown uniform, gleaming cuffs and complement of weaponry were another story.

Earl handed over papers while noting the cop's name on the badge. "What was the problem, Officer Sugarbaker?"

"Stand by!" he told Earl or the police dispatcher that he was also speaking to. Examining the papers, he replied, "No problem really, Mr. Nailor, you pulled out kind of quick back there, coming out of the Evergreen Terrace apartments. Not a biggie." He tipped his head like it almost wouldn't matter.

"Evergreen Terrace, sir?" Earl's heart rate shot up as the cop spoke, recalling his speeding on leaving Hector's place. "You sure you have the right car?"

"Oh, yes! You're that guy." The trooper's medium-dark complexion matched his puke-brown uniform. And his eyes were all business, but he had that dumb, "Du-uh" grin, like a simpering monkey. "No big," he repeated, grinning away.

Okay, maybe he speeded but no serious law got broken, so Earl figured the officer was either a stupid asshole or very cunning, often not much to choose between those anyway.

"Officer, I'm just curious, but who follows someone for miles for pulling out of a parking lot?"

It was meant as lighthearted remark, but the officer shot back, "You almost hit me." He glared at Earl with that same monkey grin of his. Uh-oh! Earl got worried. "I don't see any evidence of insurance, either," added the cop.

"It's right there," Earl almost raised his voice. "Right on the registration. At the bottom."

"This is an out-of-state registration."

Earl almost wised-off, saying instead, "An official stamp isn't enough?" He amazed himself by keeping his head.

"Well, I got you on speeding. Fifty-eight in a 30 zone."

"Naah. Really?" Earl gasped as if innocently surprised.

With both hands on his gun belt, the officer appeared to think. "Tell you what, Mr. Nailor, sir, put away your things and please step out of the car." Oh, what the hell now! Earl yelled in his mind. Then, he put away his papers to comply.

Sugarbaker pointed to the curbside grass as he scanned Earl head to toe. "Just go up there. Go ahead." So, Earl did it. "Just go ahead right up there, next to my car." He studied Earl stepping along the grass. Then, nonchalant as could be, Sugarbaker opened the back door of his cruiser. "Go ahead, have a seat!" he told Earl in the friendliest voice, like he was granting a favor by allowing him into the cruiser's back seat. Earl considered it for a few seconds, and instead, he sat down with both legs outside the car, wondering what to do and say while taking note of numerous dents and scrapes on the grate separating the cruiser's front and back seat. One gouge was two inches deep, so that was one royally pissed off prisoner. Sugarbaker was very experienced, and cool. He worked in a way that people incarcerate themselves voluntarily and thank him for it! Earl also realized the back seat was so tight, there was no space to move once the door closed.

Standing in knee-high jackboots with that phony grin of his, Sugarbaker waited to slam the door shut and blocked any opening to run. Earl got a terrifying sensation, his heart began thumping inside while he processed this loss of freedom and control over his life. At least with the door still open and not completely inside yet, he could choose to bolt. Earl asked as calmly as possible, "So, what is going on here, officer? Am I under arrest?"

"Oh, no!" he laughed. "Of course not. Please, just get in, just for a minute, please, Mr. Nailor."

The cop was on a "phishing" expedition, he could think straight enough to comprehend that much. He would need to arrest Earl and search him to find the pills, which were legal anyway…so all he had to do was stay cool himself, and soon he'd be out of this. If not, it might be real trouble. Earl swung one of his legs into the compressed back seat, and prayed he could endure the hassle unscathed legally or psychologically. Financially, he was already down hundreds on the speeding. Plus a few grand worth of scuba gear and all the time lost. So Earl pulled the other foot inside and the door slammed shut with a weighty clunk, sealed like a safe.

Sugarbaker got in the front seat and began making small talk. "I'm sorry for the delay, Mr. Nailor. Standard Procedure in such cases. With the out-of-state papers. And all."

Earl observed him through the cross-hatched steel grate. Next, two more police cars with lights ablaze, pinned Earl's car in front and on the side. Some crazy Standard Procedure! Streams of terror and adrenaline pumped throughout. "What is happening?" he mumbled through the waffle grate. Except the weasel cop did not seem to hear because he popped out of the car to meet with the arriving cops.

In a minute, Sugarbaker returned to the door and opened it for Earl. "Thank you, Mr. Nailor. You can step out." Now he spoke in a very agreeable voice. Thank God! Earl thought, finally a good sign. "Do you mind if we check your car?" the cop inquired. "Then you can go."

To Earl's disgust, first more phishing games, though! He played Earl like a cat with a mouse. "Check? For what, sir?"

"Your friend back over at the Evergreen Terrace, Hector Arce, got so doped up he collapsed right in the parking lot." he told Earl. "Almost died. Hope the drug deal was worth it." The new cops joined them at the curbside. "The other news is bad, too, I got an alcohol whiff in the car. Tight places are ideal for detecting alcohol without breathalyzers." Then Earl recalled the beer he had at Hector's, and almost screamed as the cop exchanged laughs with the other cops making a wall around him. Hairless and brown like a mudbrick, Sugarbaker added, "But the *worst* news is that you're under arrest for the distribution of controlled substances, to your friend."

"Wha-at?"

After reading Earl his rights, the cop told him, "You got recorded handing pills to Mr. Arce, which he ingested before collapsing, the same pills in your car and the same ones you dropped in the parking lot." Then, he asked with that impish grin, "We can help you, if you help yourself, and tell us what your deal was with distributing the pills there?"

"If there were pills, officer, I assure you they were legal ones, or somebody stole them." Those were the only things

Earl could think of saying.

"So you admit you had controlled substances which may have found their way into somebody else's hands?" he spoke as though providing another convenient service.

"No. Of course not." Earl gave his answer more thought. "I'm not saying anything."

"Those drugs almost killed Hector. Your friend. It took two teams of paramedics to save him. You don't feel bad?"

Earl didn't respond except to say, "It wasn't my doing if he collapsed." God-damn *me!* God-damn *fool!* Earl yelled at himself, crammed into the cruiser's back seat with this waffle grate one foot in front of his face. And, pretty soon it would be bars of rolled steel up in his face, dammit! Hector, that moron must have taken many more pills than he saw! God-dammit, he hated himself for stupidity and carelessness and trusting in anyone! Even with recordings it would be hard to prove what was passed in the bag, or if they were over-the-counter meds or even candies, but Hector and Weenie could testify against him. For a few hundred-worth of gear this now explodes into ridiculous trouble! Maybe someone informed too—must've been Dee, or the Weenie. Or the Black shopping-cart beggar, maybe *he* was the area's undercover narc, freakin' dirty old devil. Or, maybe *he*—stinky shopping-cart pusher—was the neighborhood drug dealer just protecting his turf, the Weenie was his partner, and they plotted to frame him for everything! Smart. Big Weenie devil, he was even worse than he looked!

So, it could have been anybody overlooking the parking lot who called the cops. However he looked at the situation, it was careless, and stupid. As Sugarbaker took his time with paper work in the front seat, most passers-by slowed down to rubbernecking speed, and peered at "Earl the Moron," shoe-horned into his wire cage like a caught animal. All Earl could think and dream about was diving again, gliding around free, loving those wonderful feelings of sliding effortless through nature's beauty as far as possible from lights or pavements.

***

Hector recovered. However, Earl ended up in ridiculous legal trouble, and required a commensurately-priced lawyer who managed to put him into a new drug program, where he at last succeeded in getting the proper drug therapy. Finding the correct solutions for him was often an extensive exercise of trial and error, although normally his problems were due to stupidity—ugh, wrong choices!—that was obvious here. Dee and neighbors, Weenie or homeless Black guy, not even Hector had much to do with it. Living was 99% on him, not on folks with tiny fractions of a tiny fraction in comparison! As the lone common denominator with a perfect attendance record for life, he was invariably his own original influencer for whatever was happening in life just by doing or not doing something; and thereby causing a reaction from others to do or not do what they would—nobody but Earl could be 100% responsible for that!

***

Months passed before Earl found out that maybe Hector

installed a few too many security systems, and was claiming that spy devices were planted in his car and truck, as well as in his electronics, the satellite TV receivers in particular.

On one occasion he became terribly angry that his game was blacked out due to a conspiracy to make more money! So he sent threatening emails to the satellite TV president about spy bugs recording him at home. Dee was concerned enough to record Hector ranting to himself. Earl learned all this when they invited him back get a deal " he couldn't refuse" on their dive gear. He hesitated, recalling the family's Jesus-bent and fresh off the neighborhood sting. But now he felt destined to get what he came for, and didn't mind seeing the bird, either.

When he arrived, Hector could not wait to play the tape Dee recorded of him talking or acting crazy, and he laughed heartily at himself. It went, "Oh, OK, no. Yes. Insurance is all right…the car thing, that's gonna cost plenty, though…sure. Yeah, but I'm fine there, too, OK, not fine, but we gonna kill the *beeetch* anyway!" Hector kept laughing and listening, as did Earl. "Money, money. Work, money. Work, work… God. That kid is a Weenie, too? Sure…the new wiring systems are some real nosy *beeetches*, bro-man, never seen nothin…not that it was illegal like these other things, just people may get the wrong idea. That other guy was no good, bro, wasn't he?"

The tape went on for hours with the same "word salad," much like the unfiltered thoughts of many good or otherwise sane people, Earl guessed! Hector had a wider paranoia, and above all, he had the type of ego fiercely devoted to being or to proving himself right somehow. Even in the midst of this self-inflicted calamity, he insisted and Earl finally conceded, that most digital electronics can (or already were) informing on their users, and should be swept for bugs, though all were easily breached by hackers and the goverment, anyway! So, it wasn't clear how much was true or Hector's imagination, but it was treatable with the proper therapy and meds.

Dee brought the bird to perch on Earl's shoulder, and he loved that, nutcracker beak, and all!

"Now I play the tape for everyone!" proclaimed Hector.

"Are you sure that's a good idea?" Earl laughed.

"It shows how much I needed good drugs!"

"Um, okay… If that's what you want people to know." In a way, he understood how Hector's paranoia took root. He specialized in wiring advanced security systems and became overworked and overstressed with nobody to talk to because of the company's repressive policies. Earl finally asked about the work situation itself, which started them on this journey.

"Yes, things are good at work, too," he reported. "Turns out the boss' daughter has the same thing as me!" He slapped the table top. "Now they give her drugs. And she's fine, too! They love me again. So…it's real good for us. I even gave up drinking beer! Just drugs now, dude!" he boasted, and raked his hair back to let it drape down however. Nice to see some things about him hadn't changed. And, he was quite proud of his "legal drug user" status! A big ol' flag-waver, in fact!

Dee came to the table and wrapped her arms around her burly spouse, declaring, "Thank God for the right doctor too!" She fixed Hector's hair where raking it back messed it up.

The words echoed in Earl's mind, Thank heaven! Then, Dee smoothed back the bird's crest, who had already gone to sleep on Earl's shoulder; Earl also smoothed over Samantha's lush crest, then all watched as the now-awake Samantha eyed Earl doing so with her full consent, which in return made him respect—if not love—the gorgeous animal for accepting and trusting him so. "A new companion like this could be terrific for me," he thought out loud.

Weenie exclaimed, "She never lets me get that close!"

Hector changed the subject. "We can't forget, Adam has a little present for you."

Weenie bounced off the couch and plopped a big canvas seabag on the kitchen table for Earl. "Go ahead, open it."

Earl tilted his head as if suspicious. "This is not another drug deal, is it?" he half-joked.

They all had a chuckle, and Earl started opening the bag while Dee spoke, "We were sorry about the problems… You wanted the stuff more than anyone, you deserve it."

"Sure. Wow, yeah." Earl slowly recognized the contents. "Looks good…" He pulled out the scuba mask and regulator, entangled with the dive computer, gauges and twisted hoses like drawing entrails out of the bag.

"They're all yours, bro," Weenie told him.

Suddenly Earl was feeling on the joyous side, they were the most important and expensive pieces of the equipment. "That is good stuff! What we be talkin' about!" Earl ignored his fear of somehow losing the gear again, or of this being a cruel joke, and allowed himself the freedom to be genuinely grateful and excited about diving!

Dee told him, "You can thank Jesus." Her face beamed.

Earl wouldn't think of it but nodded anyway, of course.

Weenie explained, "We knew how you wanted to dive all the time, and thought that if anybody would…" He paused to drag the tank over, too. "You'd get the most out of it."

"With the trouble," added Hector, "we figured you may not have much to deal. But, I still wanted to make that right, what went wrong… So, who knows, start a diving school!"

"Free!" Weenie announced. "Whadda'ya think of that?"

"Our gift," Dee said again.

The bird squawked. Earl figured he'd have to undergo at least some degree of proselytizing, which was still worth it.

"Free and clear!" Weenie clapped Earl squarely but hard on the shoulder, so hard that Earl felt a flash of anger before Weenie added with good intent, "Didn't expect that, did ya!"

"Wow. This is so nice of you. Free? Wow," he repeated.

Hector hugged Dee, and observed, "Guess The Big Guy Upstairs knows how to get things done right."

Weenie quipped, "You couldn't have hoped for more!" In truth, Earl was moved especially by Weenie, whose round face was rosy with big blue eyes clearly pleased about what he was doing, and left Earl almost speechless.

"Agh… I wasn't even thinking… Or dreaming anything like this," is all he could say about the gear, their generosity, the bird, and everything else. This beat his old deal to score all the gear for $3 worth of pills! Minus his legal fees!

After extended visiting time, he bid Hector, Dee and the Weenie warm Good-byes. The bird rubbed her bountiful crest across his cheeks and lips several times, and he headed to the parking lot with his bag of dive treasure in a fold-up cart!

They were fine folks, as good as they come—forgetting

their religiosity! No doubt their religious beliefs played a key role in why they were honorable, well-meaning people—but the rituals or religiosity itself, not much to do with it.

Earl could only dream ahead about his glorious next day of diving. Except for outer space, he figured, it was as close to escaping terra firma, or truly getting away from it all!

On the way out, the Black beggar pushed his shopping cart which was spilling over with his "wordly possessions," across the exit. The old guy's eyes seemed to twinkle; bright and almost bagel-sized, they shone like hi-beams but for their dark center points. His broken cartwheel continued its crazy spinning and squealing as he proceeded to cross Earl's path, singing away, "Ain't singin for Spuds! Ain't dyin' for dopes, Dope! I'm just a miner for a heart of hope, Dope! Then save the Spuds, Spud!"

The guy's eyes were so vibrant and electric that sparking energy seemed to shoot out and dance around like a different being inhabited his broke-down body. "Git along, brother…" he urged. "G'od luck now," he added like he was in charge of everything. He might as well have been for all the sense that he or life made!

Watching him push the cart from behind, then passing in front of him, Earl saw a carboard sign stuck to his backside, with the words, "DRIVER IN THE REAR," plus a couple of crazy arrows, one pointed ahead and one pointed back Earl's way.

Definitely driving from the rear! Worth a farewell laugh, too! Earl didn't know why, he couldn't explain it, but he also couldn't escape the feeling that the homeless guy had at least something to do with all that happened from the beginning when Earl was lost, and almost hit him on the tracks. Usually unseen or overlooked, the guy popped up anywhere, out of nowhere, as though always in the background and close, like there was always this "driver in the rear" around.

IT IS WRITTEN...

TENDER CONCRETE

(Don't Make Me Squeal!)

Woman jilts her fiancé and arranges a ménage à trois with a new friend and her husband.

*J*ordan Temple wanted to lie around a crackling Christmas Eve fire with his wife, but Bill Dorman needed help, and begged him to meet at a local dive bar, *The Plow and Stars*. It was on the way home, one of these dark pubs with rough-hewn wood, sawdust and peanut shells strewn over the floor as décor. Bill's fiancée just gave him the axe, and his severed head rolled down into this dump. Jordan gathered the rest of him hadn't eaten for days. His pants were falling off, his head bobbed, and sticky brown saliva collected in the corners of his mouth from knocking back too many Guinness Stouts.

Fragrant laurel and Christmas garlands adorned the pub walls. The entrance featured a prominent Nativity display in the finest barnyard tradition—plastic Jesus, Mary and Joseph surrounded by sheep, jackasses, some "wise men" and even pigs.

Everyone had a smile but Bill, who couldn't escape his tortured emotions on the worst eve of the year to feel alone.

"My condolences," Jordan told him.

"I'm beyond consoling," he replied with a sucking noise. Jordan wasn't sure whether Bill misunderstood, or was being insulting. "I'm past 'consolences,' whatever that word was."

Bill's fiancée was a Swedish blond named Olo. He knew them through his wife Maria, and they seemed to be a strong couple. Now they were just another yank on the chain of long sad experience—tra-la di-dah!—he joked to himself.

Both quit cigarettes which Jordan appreciated about Bill, yet spending precious time here was questionable. He prayed that Bill wasn't angling for help to get his girl back. By now he probably alienated everyone else, and he did beg. Besides those, Jordan's main reasons for coming tonight were selfish. Everybody experienced their "share" of adversity in this life, but Jordan hoped to experience what he imagined being "his share" of adversity *through others*, by proxy—as if it were even possible! He visited folks in hospitals, or down on their luck, he volunteered, recycled, donated, like doing so would lessen the chance or severity of any misfortune hitting him! It was no worse than other superstitions and worked thus far in his life, so it wasn't harmful. As superstitions go, his may help, in fact, especially if the cosmos was just some infinite "ledger-based" system, which many people believed. Jordan also tried learning everything he could from the mistakes of others; never did it bother him that bad things happening to them often helped him feel better about himself. What good was feeling bad as well? He changed it into a plus. Someone should! Bill's pain made him value his 25 blessed years with Maria all the more. Yes, they were grateful, but proud, too.

Who decided Bill's break-up was bad, anyway? Because he thought so? If it happened, chances are it's for the best.

"Loving Olo...that was such a habit," Bill seemed to be telling himself. "Then, you realize...she's gone. Just...gone. I been sick in my stomach. Seein' double... Her? She knows it's prob'ly the only thing too."

According to Bill, he dumped her first, before they were really over, in order to save some face. "Good for you," said Jordan facetiously. But Bill thought he was serious. He went off about how courage was the most valuable quality he had in life, courage to face the inevitable, and charge back ahead again! Jordan didn't agree or disagree, he left a blank stare on his face. Grief, guilt, fear, they were everywhere, but courage was a No Show. He was like something screwed into a tight socket, where no power could flow through.

Jordan whiffed a charburger with fries going to another customer, and considered Bill's condition. "You look like you could use a good meal," he suggested. "For your courage."

"A-ach, no way. Eatin' reminds me of Olo...we always ate togeth'r..." His head wobbled like a bobblehead atop his stool. "But, itza funny thing..." To prevent slurring, Bill tried forcing his lips into the right shapes for pronouncing words. "Didn't think of me having cour'ge...til lately. Risking it all in a bid'ness, letting myself fall in love. Taking root in life," he announced, lifting his fist a few inches. "Now, she don't want it." Dropping his fist like dead weight. "She *grew up!*" he said uglily. "Now, I ain't good 'nuff... Ur smart 'nuff... Or nothin!" With the ugliest snarl, he reached out his glass in a mock toast. "Cheers, to cour'ge! No, wait... To love. Yeah.

Here's to love!" He chugged a half-pint of Guinness. Jordan noted its descent in a string of lumps through his neck.

Bill swayed on the stool while one large lump ascended, and he belched vengefully as if expelling the sick from deep within. Large brown eyes bulged out, glazed over, and dried saliva around his lips formed little dark crusts. In the fluid of his eyeballs Jordan saw reflected the people and things going on around them. Poor slob. He must be numb at last, demons flooded, all his lights punched out, except Jordan was wrong. Bill watched him askance as if feeling his thoughts, not like a dummy but with his broad bony shoulders pinched up, and small head bobbing.

"Why you lis'ning to me?" he said in a hostile voice. "Ya don' give a damabout me and Olo." Burp! "Yur jus' an ass'ole sit'n there grateful it's snot hap'ning to you. Ur is it b'cause this is Chris'mus, and you wanna be human for once?" Burp!

"Neither." Jordan told him the truth. "I do care… In my way." It was good enough to give him pause. "The reason is to let you know that Bill is OK, no matter what happens. Bill is OK." Jordan had a thin smile, and kept staring true.

Desperate to connect and to trust in something again, the fine muscles around Bill's eyes began relaxing. He appeared to separate Jordan from his grief, and accept that making Olo or himself to be wrong for anything did not matter to Jordan.

A couple folk singers were getting set to play in front of a giant evergreen draped in silver tinsel and flickering colored lights. The bar started crowding up with smiling people, some women, mostly men. The only women in this place were the type that could handle really drunk men.

It was disappointing to see Bill lighting a cigarette with hands shaking. "I quit," he reminded Jordan, and signaled the bartender for a beer. Jordan sipped on his with a disagreeable stare. "But, you're right," Bill sighed, registering his friend's disapproval. "I should never let 'er get to me completely." He screwed the butt into the ashtray with a disgusted sound, and shoved it away. Maybe he would perk up after all, and Jordan got an even greater feeling of well-being.

On stage the two guitarists started to play crisp and loud acoustic music, a cross of hillbilly and folk. Right away they caught on with the crowd by trading guitar licks, and singing an amusing song about lies. The crowd clapped and joined in a chorus of the word "Lies! Lies!" They sang it loud, with a happy hatred, as if to drive the idea out of this place, and they could together. Jordan joined them as Bill looked incredulous and wiped a sleeve across his mouth. Jordan laughed, hands clapping, not caring about his trouble. The song finished and neither spoke. Instead, both noticed the cigarette smoldering in the ashtray, so Bill pounded it down until it died. Another song began.

Bill drank his new beer, then he leaned over and blurted in a crude voice, "I'm sure she was giving it away… Bitch."

He almost fell off the stool.

Jordan pulled away in case Bill fell in his direction. "Do you know for sure if she was?"

"She had to be. She wanted more than me." He paused, adding, "A-ach, what's the difference… Itchy broad."

"But, did Olo say that she still loved *you?*" Jordan went straight to the bottom line.

"She says, 'She does…but, she doesn't.' Which means No." Bill was right, of course. "I mean, if she still loved me," he added, "we could work on it…renew somehow, y' know?"

Jordan didn't think that was necessarily true. But the guy was trying to be objective so he didn't bring up circumstances. Bill surprised him, though, he was quite honest with himself, he had warmth, and was trying to be strong considering what he was going through. Despite inebriation, he communicated those qualities. Jordan wasn't sure he wouldn't be in twice as bad shape if something happened to Maria and him. But, he couldn't imagine anything they wouldn't be able to work out at this stage. If history counts for anything, they would never reach such a desperate point.

Bill couldn't stop brooding. "The heart's been ripped out of everything." He lifted his face, and caught his reflection in the dull wall mirror behind the bar; a moment later, he shook his head at the likeness. "God… Gotta pull myself together." He searched Jordan's face as if for confirmation. "What's the big deal, anyway? Aren't thousands of couples on the planet going through this same crap right now?" Bill stared at both of their reflections in the dull mirror as though it was one of the most profound thoughts ever uttered. Except, all around them was nothing but happy people celebrating.

Bill wiggled down from the stool, and trudged to the rest room. Meanwhile, Jordan asked the bartender about the pub's name, and found out the *Plow and Stars* was the Irish name for the Big Dipper constellation, as well as the emblem of the Irish Citizen Army, precursor of the IRA. True to himself, he tried to learn from everything. The Big Dipper, he chuckled, that was appropriate for Bill's big bender!

When Bill returned his hair was combed, mouth cleaned, and face washed. He didn't smell too stinky anymore, either. Now, his 3-day beard looked almost good, in a rugged Wild West way. Still, he could not get Bill's new nickname out of his head—the Big Dipper! Funny, too, because there wasn't anything "big" about Bill except the bender he was on!

"Y'know," Bill said, "it wou'n't bother me so much she was spreadin' herself around…if I still thought she couldn't get closer to someone else. She opened my eyes way too late to do anything." He finished with a helpless palm-up gesture while smiling at somebody behind Jordan.

Jordan turned to see a woman at the end of the bar with henna hair, smiling back in their direction. Bill had the deep brown eyes plus a welcoming smile that seemed to both catch and receive another's. His complexion was a light tan shade and pleasingly smooth.

"Very friendly," Jordan remarked.

"How could she resist?" he answered. He believed it.

"I meant that you were 'very friendly'," Jordan clarified himself.

"No, I'm just a tease," he replied with a smug look. He did think a lot of himself, though, which made it easier to be less sympathetic about his loss. The musicians kept playing. Everybody kept enjoying themselves.

Jordan had to go to the bathroom so he excused himself. It was a shame about Bill's relationship, he concluded while holding himself over the urinal. Just another yank on the old chain! He grinned at his rare outbreak of potty humor.

Washing his hands, Jordan continued to studying himself in the mirror and to consider more about Maria. It could never be over with them, even if the worst happened and marriage stopped working. They had far too many happy loving times between them. The truth about love was that love was just a chance. People would do what they wanted most whether in love relationships or not; love forced people to grow which wasn't only the chance but the wondrous part—growing, and finding more desire to love each other, it's not the love itself. Love and loving were choices we must *want* to keep making for ourselves, one's own satisfaction, sometimes moment to moment, he believed it.

Jordan went back out, repeating to himself, "The *desire to love* is the key," so he could share his thought with Maria.

He found Bill talking to that friendly henna-haired girl. When Jordan sat down Bill came back over with a smile, and Jordan almost suggested that he invite the new girl out for a meal. "You look much better. Finally pulling that giant brick out of your ass?" Jordan needled him with good intent but his friend scowled like it was a serious affront—as if to say, Excuse me? Or like he may take a swing at Jordan. "So, did you make 'contact' with her?" he was quick to ask.

Bill's face naturally relaxed and he replied with a smile, "Maybe." He tried to play it down but the word still came out hopeful. "I thought she might like a free pack of used butts."

"And…what?"

"She quit, too!" he announced.

"Great!"

"That's what I said!" A pause followed. "She's not that

bad at all. Is she?" Jordan didn't want to answer his question so Bill answered it for himself. "Not like Olo, though."

"No," Jordan agreed. "Different."

Bill almost looked surprised, then amused. They enjoyed a few more minutes of lively tunes and camaraderie as Jordan itched to go. The beers were done and neither ordered more. When Jordan put out his hand to shake, Bill stared at it first; the next second he grabbed it for a good shake. "I'd be happy if you and Maria came to my place for dinner soon."

Moisture in Bill's eyes glimmered. His expression was a warm one but best of all, showed healing. Holding the handshake, Jordan put his other arm around Bill and for moments they were as close friends. He helped Jordan feel great about spending this important time with him, and for going now.

The friendly woman wandered over, glancing their way. Bill held out his arm to her. "You know…" he spoke with an empty look, and didn't finish his thought or forgot it; instead he released a weak sigh and admitted, "Wow… I'm hungry."

Jordan and the girl grinned at one another. Bill stared up at his friend with almost pleading eyes and inspired Jordan to make a shrugging I-Don't-Know motion; then, he presented henna girl over to Bill with one hand, and Bill back to her.

Jordan was quite content and anxious to get home, so all bid Good-bye and wished each other most Happy Holidays.

"Thought you had a boyfriend…" he overheard Bill say to the henna-girl on his way out. But the only thought Jordan had, what he wanted most this Christmas Eve was just to kiss his wife 'til she glowed in the dark.

When he got home everything was still. He had to wait.

CLIMAX

Last-minute Christmas shopping was all he could think of. Or, an emergency. Maria was so dependable, Jordan could always count on her to tell him where she was, plus this was Christmas Eve. Crappy sensations filled him from the bottom up. It wasn't a shopping thing, all the stores closed at 6. Then, he could not recall if he told her why he was going to be late himself, that almost never happened, either.

Jordan checked the house, messages, inboxes, called her cell, nothing. Called her mom, friends, the neighbors, no one knew where she went, and her car was in the garage. Instead of panicking, Jordan started a fire. Then, voices outside!

Thank God, Maria, with somebody else. Keys jangled in the door, and his cheerful wife appeared with shopping bags, plus none other than Bill Dorman's ex-fiancée, the adorable blond Olo—she of the large silky lips, delicate nose and slim figure with almost no hips. He was relieved, but also wanted to be angry.

"Hey, honey," greeted Maria. "You remember Olo, Bill Dorman's fiancée?"

"Former fiancée," she corrected his wife.

"Former fiancée." Maria touched Olo's hand.

Jordan was thankful, surprised, irritated. Then confused. He thought it was to be their own holiday time together, and he wanted to get naked and sexual. "So, what are you gals up to this Christmas Eve? Last minute shopping?"

"Oh, we're just having a little affair!" Maria answered in a joking manner, and laughed.

Olo laughed, too. "So, we are? It is official, then?" She moved closer to Maria with a sizzling smile and Maria threw back her thick brown hair. They had to be kidding, right?

Jordan also smiled at Olo's waif-like body so close to his wife's, then he got a definite feeling they were serious, or else why kid around? So ironic after where Jordan had been!

"Bill didn't tell you I was bi?" Olo asked with an amused glance. She had huge ice-blue eyes, and bobbed up pixie cut to go with her large inviting lips.

"Never came up. Sorry…" Jordan kept staring into Olo's engulfing blue eyes which she welcomed. "Bisexual? No. We would have remembered that, I'm pretty sure!"

His mind switched—or jumped the tracks—to having a threesome with Olo and Maria, in front of their new roaring Christmas fire! Maybe she liked multiples, and Bill didn't. He almost mentioned Bill but that might backfire, so instead he said, "If I could remember you are Swedish, I'd remember that you were bi!"

Jordan's heart beat fast as he dared imagine a threesome coming true, and fantasized about her with Maria. It might be perfect, adultery with no guilt or consequences if all agreed! Such an outrageous possibility never occurred to him before! Still, Christmas Eve, the crackling fire, come on!

But, if they were having a Lesbian affair—big surprise, Jordan might not be any better off than Bill! No threesomes, maybe no nothing ever again! Just a big chunk of coal in his Christmas stocking! Everything looked up in the air while he revolved the possible outcomes, another crossroad, and never more unsure of himself than this moment when the meaning of his future and past life with Maria seemed to hang in the balance.

Maria had downcast eyes as though she had something to tell him but didn't want to. She was wearing her comfy jeans and "Dancing Santa" sweater; Olo had a knee-length flannel skirt, cashmere top and blue stockings with shiny black boots. She and Jordan watched Maria empty the shopping bag full of fruits and cheese with long auburn hair cascading around her shoulders. Olo's eyes pinged back and forth between the two of them, and Jordan. Something was definitely going on here. Then a lopsided apple fell out of the bag and rolled to a stop right in front of Jordan as though presenting itself.

"Well, listen, girls," he announced, "I guess we will duck upstairs, shed these clothes. And be right back." He gave his wife a quick kiss on the lips, figuring if she had something to say she would follow him. But seconds after he left the room they were giggling. Not wanting to be found eavesdropping, Jordan headed upstairs but only reached the third step before reversing direction to check the mail. On top was a thin letter from their lawyers, which he ripped open.

It was a huge bill for their zoning application, and ticked him right off. There was something else from the lawyers, a holiday card, compounding the irritation.

In the hall, he heard Maria ask Olo, "What are you doing Saturday, suppose you're going out with this new guy?"

"He has a family thing. Want to look for some perfume?"

"Sure. Maybe. I could use a new scent."

"Yeah, I need a new scent."

The sink faucet went on. "Still haven't been able to get a picture of his dick for you." What an astonishing thing for his wife to just come out and say! So, that's why her phone was propped up on the bureau!

The faucet spray stopped, and footsteps fast approached him. He hid behind the door.

"I have enough 'big dick' pics," stated Olo.

"I'll get it. He's not *huge*. Over seven inches...excellent girth, though, you know what I mean!" She laughed. "That's what keeps me coming!" She laughed.

"I am covered. I have my collection of literature, too."

"Oh, he doesn't mind," said his wife.

"I feel a little weird. Won't he ask?"

"He won't care. I put the boobs in his face and he don't ask many questions." Maria was right about that!

"What about the condoms?"

"I'm not fertile," said Maria. "And he's clean. You said you were, too, so we'll just do it before your period."

"Well, we won't worry about birth control, either. He'll love that."

"What man doesn't?"

He'd heard enough. Feeling whole and masculine again, Jordan returned as soon as he could to stoke the fire in his big lumberjack shirt. All enjoyed sweet fruits, wine and cheeses in front of the tree. It didn't seem like Olo had another place she would rather be, and Maria was pleased to have her. She hadn't welcomed someone else's company this way for years so Jordan wasn't about to object. Maybe she was feeling the same things as him! Firelight reflected across the surrounding parlor windows.

His wife's face had an adventurous glow while even her grays caught a touch of radiant firelight. All agreed that just lounging on the plush rug and cushions by the fireplace was perfect. They shared enthusiastic conversation and laughter.

Several times Olo shifted position and cracked her thighs open to flash Jordan inside her skirt. His wife got a hair-band and smoothed her hair back while expanding her chest, then she smiled at Olo, then over at Jordan, which also caused him to smile. After the eavesdropping, he didn't believe his wife was going Lesbian on him, but if no one would address these blatant sexual signals, he had to. "So, girls, is this some kind of an…an attraction thing here?" He motioned around to the three of them. Flames and lights flashed in off the windows.

"I don't know," answered Olo with a suggestive stare at him, then Maria; light played off Olo's fine blond hair so it shined with a strawberry hue. "Is it?"

Maria snapped the elastic band around her hair. "Jordy, Olo likes us," she told him. "A lot. Know what I mean?" She finished tying the hair in a soft floppy bun. Then grinned.

"Um, yes. I think so. I feel…I think we feel something, too. Don't we, honey?" Jordan grinned back at his amazing wife. The raw excitement of such a fantasy coming true was tough to control. Olo's legs weren't open but weren't closed, either. Her glimmering lips were part open, and luscious. She leaned away with both arms behind her and palms flat on the rug, waiting for further reactions from them.

Maria put her hand on Jordan's knee, explaining, "I was

going to bring this up when we were alone. But, it kind of all came together tonight." She threw her palms up, helpless.

Olo got closer and smiled as Jordan stirred the fire. "So, does this fulfill one of your fantasies?" she asked.

"Me? Sure." Jordan thought about Bill, all messed up at the bar. "What about you, Olo?"

"Oh, me? I'm a good girl… But, I admit, yes, sometimes I like a wicked naughty game."

"Oh… So, what is that?"

"Before I say what…"

Maria interrupted, "Oh, you know, your heart is always with that Marcel."

"Oh, yes," Olo agreed. "Marcel loved torturing me with pleasure! Oh, God, I could not wait for him to tie me up and chew and screw my pussy all night." Olo had this wild-eyed grin. "Ooooh…" She finished with an "I'm-At-The-End-Of-My-Rope" expression.

"Hmm, sounds like…um, wonderful!" he observed, and both ladies burst into giggles. "Look out!" exclaimed Jordan. "The lid is off!"

The women prepared themselves in the bedroom. Jordan browsed Maria's fashion magazines, fantasizing himself into arousal while they completed their girl stuff. There was some indistinct conversation then they appeared again—Olo wore a silk teddy, Maria a long see-through nightshirt and creamy soft breasts swinging inside, both ladies fluffy and delightful smelling, delicious curvy shapes. The magazine went flying. The fire crackled madly, flooding the parlor with flames and flickering shadows waving across the walls. They all helped with the pull-out bed for this blazing hot time in front of the tree! No "Baby Jesus" fairy tale, but a true life Christmas-In-the-Manger scene—from Playboy or Hustler!

Jordan only had one nagging hesitancy about doing this, the small matter of possible diseases. Olo appeared pristine, though, and always dressed impeccably, so while they didn't know her well, she was unikely to have anything. And Maria must've covered that with her already; it was hard to believe she wouldn't so he tried to forget about bringing it up now!

The two women lounging on the pillows gave Jordan an enormous erection. He stood beside them as Maria took the lead, wrapping her fingers around his member to make a fist, and with a squeeze dragged Jordan to the edge of the pull-out sofa in front of Olo, who almost averted her gaze. Olo said, "I want to grab those." She seized Jordan's testes, and rolled them in her hand like a pair of dice. "I love sucking on balls." So she did. And Maria sucked his member at the same time. Jordan swooned while he reached around to fondle both their chests and other love places.

Jordan wasn't sure what he liked more—Maria's round hips and skinny waist or Olo's dainty figure with slight hips. Both were equally exciting! So he grabbed and massaged nice big handfuls of each. But, if he had to choose one over again, Maria's skinny waist and rounder hips would still be it; those curves defined womanhood to him. "Honey, what would you like...for me to kiss Olo?" he said.

Maria responded by embracing her friend. "Please do," she told her husband.

"Yes. Please," said Olo, returning Maria's embrace and

extending her other arm for Jordan.

Passions flared when he kissed Olo. Her lips were sweet tasting and their large size felt cushion-perfect, sliding freely all over his. Maria kissed Jordan more lustfully than she had in some time, and she did the same with Olo. Both girls took their clothes off. Olo's ankle bracelet glinted in the firelight as she parted her long legs shyly and leaned back, compelling Jordan toward her.

He kissed and hugged Olo, cuddling his arm around her and cupping her slick mons. She gripped his shaft to suck it a lot before climbing on top; Maria kissed them both when Olo settled down to guide him up in there. She welcomed Jordan the whole way while Maria and Jordan kissed as though they couldn't kiss enough and never had before.

Olo started a rapid grinding and jamming rhythm against his loins. "Oooh, that is wicked love! God baby! God!" And a moment after, steaming hotness streamed over and around his shaft. "Wicked love!" she screeched. "You devil lover!"

"Go for it, Olo!" cheered Maria. "He'll screw that pussy good! He loves to be underneath!" For good measure, Maria draped both breasts on his face, all but smothering him while Olo's continued being firmly massaged in each of his hands.

"You devil! You hottie! You devil!" Olo wailed.

The girls kissed more. Maria was way into this, rooting Jordan on, "Nice, baby, nice! Doing it proud, baby, screwing the hell out of her! Go ahead, you know you wanted it!" He was astounded by his wife's enthusiasm. She truly wanted it for both of them! Maybe Maria was the instigator! Shadows and light from the fire danced across their pumping bodies.

"Don't make me squeal, you fucker!" yelled Olo. "Oooh, you're making me squeal, you fucker! Ayeee! Oooh Daddy! F-kng devil you Daddy!"

Maria was laughing as she dipped her tongue into Olo's mouth and they stared in each other's eyes, kissing. This was mostly a girl-on-girl thing! With his big dick thrown in!

Jordan kissed Maria and she sat on his mouth while Olo was riding up high, calling out, "Don't make me squeal, you fucker! I dare you Daddy, Ooo-oooh! Agh-ach!" He was way down with this friction beat, orgasm building from breasts in his face, and hands fondling the others. Suddenly, she shook and shivered, then gushed forth more juicy hotness, shouting away, "So, go ahead, make me squeal, you f'k-er! Go ahead, you devil Daddy!" She yelled out in pure ecstasy, "Ay-yee-yee-ee-eehah! Yah-hee! God! Shit, God, ach! Daddy Devil, agh! Daddy lover God! Agh-agh!"

Maria rocked around his tongue, as Jordan was one big shrill sensation exploding head to toe with Olo freewheeling above. "God...fkk, damn! God...f'ck!" Then, they all came! "Agh-agh... God, I love you, Daddy, you devil f'k-kk, shit... Making me squeal this way, should be ashamed you Daddy!"

Jordan wondered about all of Olo's "Daddy" references.

"Go! Go! Do me, you dirty loving devil!" shouted Olo, continuing to ride Jordan hard, almost with a vengeance. "Oh, do like that lover, do like that Daddy, agh! Yeah—agh. Oh... Woops!"

Olo stopped mid-stroke, and covered her mouth like she was shocked. Something just screwed up. "My Lord!" she exclaimed in kind of horror. "I am sorry!" And after thinking another second, Olo climbed off Jordan fast.

"But, Olo…" gasped Maria. "My God! What is it?"

"I am soo-o sor-ry, I cannot believe what I was saying!" She held herself tight on the edge of the sofa. "God…I can't believe this." Olo closed her hand over her mouth. Then, she jumped to her feet, very agitated. "What was I saying?" Her emotional state grew more worrisome as she wrapped herself in a dark comforter, and clomped around the living room.

Jordan wasn't sure about asking, but went ahead, "Olo, is it about all that 'Daddy' stuff?"

Maria shot him a glare. So did Olo. "It's not what you're thinking…" she muttered, and plunked down in the loveseat to stare into the sizzling fire.

Maria grabbed her nightshirt and checked Jordan's eyes, as both wondered whether Olo was unstable and they should never have done this.

Jordan's phone was blinking. It was a voicemail message from Bill Dorman, of all people! Jordan already had a guilty conscience that he would learn about their tryst with Olo. But the message was, "Hey, hello, Jordan, we hooked up with her for X-mas, thanks big dog! I mean the girl from the *Plow and Stars*, and her girlfriend. Together! Believe that? Thanks for pulling my head out of the crapper. You were right, Olo was a screaming basket case. Even when things were going great she found some way to feel bad." Jordan looked at Olo on the edge of the loveseat, and thought how things seemed to go great. Until they didn't! "Perfect body, though, beautiful lips. Tight little ass, long legs, and big pretty feet. I love legs and big feet, it makes me crazy talking about…oh, shit, well…"

Olo's feet happened to be only parts of her that weren't covered by the dark comforter, and almost resembled paddle wheels they were so big! Blood-red toenails and the glittering ankle chain accented their appeal.

Perhaps Olo sensed something about the call, and began to focus Jordan's way, but he smiled like nothing at all. Bill's message continued. "I never told you the biggest thing about Olo, though. She has a serious Daddy-fixation, and you look exactly like him! It's so amazing, too!" Jordan's brain almost sprang a leak upon hearing that! He saw what he could swear was his image reflected in Olo's eyes and the fire shimmering in the background. "So, watch out if you ever happen to run into Olo! She was accused of killing her Daddy for trying to have sex with her. She was acquitted, though. Just letting you know, man, she's got a weird thing going on about you. Well, take it easy, hope you and Maria have a great holiday!"

The message finished, and although his back was turned, Olo asked him outright, "Who are you listening to? Sounded a little like my Bill."

Before he replied it occurred to Jordan that Bill Dorman already knew about Olo's desires to have sex with them, and was out to poison the well first. Even if he was not trying to spoil things he must know of Olo's desire and maybe that she was here, too, or he would not leave such a message. All this lent new meaning to her "Do me Daddy" exclamations. And also must be why Bill called Jordan to witness his misery at the bar! In fact, the entire night felt like multiple ambushes, his wife's surprise, now this about Olo, plus Bill! Jordan was just along for the rides!

Maria noted his puzzled state and said, "Dammit, Jordy, what's going on? Who was it?"

"That was Bill," he confessed. "Your Bill…" He stared at Olo. "Leaving us a nice holiday message… Of love… And how much I reminded Olo of her evil Daddy devil." Jordan almost smirked at one, then at the other woman.

Like an involuntary reaction, Maria's lower lip covered her upper lip. Olo did not appear surprised nor upset; instead, she shrugged. "What else did he say?"

Jordan sighed, reluctant to comply. "He also mentioned that you killed your father…in self-defense."

Maria's eyes reeled up. She whacked the Santa cushion and stuffed her face in it to muffle her scream. "So she killed her father—shit, you jerk!" she yelled, and then whipped the cushion at him. "He molested her, I'd do the same!"

Oh, so now *Jordan* is the bad guy! The last one to know anything—the threesome, Maria's secret desire, the incest or murder of the perp. Oh, what a Holy Night!

"I should go." Olo hopped off the chair.

"No, please." Maria jumped up, too. "What happened?"

Olo stared at Jordan. By now her face acquired an older appearance where tiny cracks in her makeup showed. "Merry Christmas," she wished them. The more Jordan looked at her big intense eyes, the more their size looked out of proportion with the rest of her; and some aspects of her appearance like the large eyes and lips and feet, now seemed on the freakish side. Olo gathered her things and withdrew to the bathroom.

Maria's mouth sagged as she slammed herself backward against the messed-up sofa bed, but neither of them objected to her leaving. He also threw himself back on the bed, noting the time, 2 a.m., projected on the ceiling. "It's Christmas."

Lying across the sofa, Jordan and Maria gazed into each other's face, so many emotions swirling, satisfaction, worry, astonishment, appreciation. They kissed for several seconds, wrapped arms around each other, contemplating the tree and the fire instead.

"It's a very Merry Christmas," she said, and they smiled at one another, cuddling tighter.

"All the holiday trimmings..." was the only comment he thought of.

The bathroom door flew open, and Olo was on the phone arguing, topless with one stocking on. "It's so disrespectful, Bill!" she raised her voice.

They popped to attention. With a narrow impatient look Olo plunked herself on the loveseat facing them, and opened her legs to roll on her other stocking, which also highlighted the outlines of her pubic cleft and caused her firm breasts to swing. Jordan massaged Maria's shoulders and thighs while they listened.

"I don't care! Screw yourself!" she shouted at Bill, and both grinned at Olo. "I don't owe you anything." She parted her legs again and also grinned; these circumstances amused her. The flames, shadows and points of colored tree lights all flickered and reflected in the windows. "No. You're wrong, I do love you, but you don't respect me." Olo had a smirk of amazement while watching Jordan and Maria react, who both smiled at her game. She smoothed out the blue stockings and dangled her perfect creamy breasts for good measure.

Jordan reclined on the sofa-bed with Maria between his spread-open legs. His massaging continued, fondling Maria's breasts from behind while they watched Olo arguing. But he secretly wanted to help Olo smooth her stockings! Thoughts of sucking her pussy while she kept quarreling on the phone also crossed his mind. His next crazy thought was doing that! With his naughtiest smile Jordan did get up to do it!

Olo was unsure but recognized the warped fun to be had and rested an outstretched leg across Jordan's shoulder, then wrapped it around the back of his head to pull his lips closer to hers, at the same time as he kissed her upper-thighs to the hot wet spot. The fight also heated up, with Olo doing a great shrew imitation, smashing Bill verbally and the pussy tasting so delicious it reminded Jordan of a honey-dipped doughnut. Bill's verbal beating and everything else seemed meaningless in comparison to Olo's loveliness which was flowing nectar.

By now she panted hard and reached her arms to Maria, who came over to kiss her bare open chest and then faced her pubis at Olo's mouth for her own pleasure. Bill kept right on screaming his nasty rant when the phone dropped to the floor, and it was neither picked up, nor turned off. Flames cracked and sparks flew as all abandoned themselves to lovemaking.

No sooner was it 4 a.m. on Christmas with Round Two in the books, when the doorbell chimed, ending their bliss.

"What in hell could that be?" Jordan exclaimed.

"Honey, let Santa in," Maria joked in a drowsy voice.

Another second later they were all knocked out of their stupors by heavy pounding. A garbled voice was audible.

"Oh, no." Olo gasped. "That sounds like Bill again."

Maria bounced out of bed.

Jordan's head jerked around in disgust. "Unbelievable." How did he not see this coming! Please! Adultery without consequences, c'mon, this kind of shit always blows back!

Maria's face pinched up, and she seemed alarmed now. "Does he own a gun?"

"No. He's not a violent person," Olo replied.

BANG! The door thumped. BANG!! "Olo! Olo! Please, baby!" It was Bill alright. "Please, baby. I love you…Jesus, baby," he called inside to Olo. "Baby, Jesus, it's Cris-mus."

"How does he know you're here?" Maria demanded. "A tracking app?"

"Or, the time we came for dinner," Olo replied. "He may have guessed, then he probably drives by and sees my car."

Maybe we should call the police," Maria suggested. "He sounds wasted. Irrational." She folded her arms. "Jordy?"

"You're probably right," Jordan answered. At the pub it was already was Day Three of Bill's Big Bender!

"No. I will talk to him," said Olo. In a flash she donned her top and panties, then answered the door. Maria followed in a full-length robe. Jordan folded up the pull-out sofa, and straightened up the room.

Bill Dorman stumbled across the threshold, a brooding little figure in the dark foyer. The Big Dipper himself! Olo cradled his cute pathetic face in her hand. Maria switched on the light, and Jordan was surprised that Bill shaved between their time at the bar and now. He looks to have showered and changed clothes too. After they kissed nicely Maria left them alone and withdrew to join Jordan on the parlor sofa where they both watched, curious, nervous and exhausted.

Olo and Bill whispered things, then embraced. Now, Olo seemed apologetic and understanding, even kittenish, as she rubbed her stocking-clad legs over Bill's trousers. More was whispered, and Bill livened up. Soon, Olo pranced back into the parlor and threw on her blouse, skirt, boots, then coat. "No way he can drive his car. I am taking him home."

Bill shuffled in behind Olo, and scanned their parlor. His eyes locked on the big cushions around the fireplace, then the wine bottles, then some sheets Jordan left hanging out of the sofa bed. Bill exhaled, as his entire self deflated again. From the tight lips and eyelids drooping with disappointment, Bill seemed to recreate what took place, while Jordan tried not to look; he was tragic. It had to be one of his worst times, but Jordan didn't care too much, Bill brought a lot on himself.

Then, like the *Plow and Stars*, when Jordan discounted Bill, he perked up and bellowed with jolly Ho-Ho! laughter. "Guess you got everything out of your systems!" He tossed his hands up in frustration and resignation, concluding, "No matter what you do, people just do what they want!"

Whether they are in love or not… Jordan finished Bill's sentence in his mind.

Olo grinned back at him and Maria. "Yeah, yeah, got all that out of our systems now… Go on, Bill, this is not a nice look for you."

"Not a nice look, Bill!" he joked. "Not nice, ho-ho!"

Bill and Olo departed in rather merry moods, snuggling arm-in-arm, and jabbing each other playfully, as Jordan and Maria waved Good-byes and thanked God for the harmless but never-to-be-repeated encounter. Maybe Olo did love him and they would reunite. Perhaps she needed to get stuff out of her system first, such as finding a look-alike of her old man to remake the bad experiences in a pleasurable way. Or gain some power over the abuse that she could never have before.

There was talking outside, then louder voices. Maria and Jordan went to the window, and saw two women waiting for Bill in the car. They must be the ones at the *Plow and Stars* he mentioned in the message. That girl with henna hair gave Jordan a friendly wave, and Maria's expression tightened up from exhaustion or annoyance.

But, it sounded like a disagreement was brewing.

"I'm going to bed," Maria huffed. She stomped upstairs.

Before she was out of sight, Jordan wondered when to ask her if she covered the subject of disease with Olo. "Say, you confirmed with Olo that she didn't have any…like…any diseases, right? Before we did this whole thing?"

"No," she replied. "Oh, she would have said something if she did, she's fine," Maria dismissed it and went upstairs.

"I know." He thought for a second, then mumbled, "But, what if she does? Did?" But, she ignored or didn't hear him.

Jordan stayed to see what was developing between Olo and the bar girls. They had more words as Bill leaned against his car. Some pushing broke out, along with curses.

Olo yelled at Bill, "You slept with the skanky bitches!"

"No!" the second girl shouted back. "*I* didn't sleep with him! She did!" Pointing to henna girl.

For a few seconds Bill hung his head like a bad boy. The instant he peeked up, Olo uncorked one huge roundhouse of punch to his head, which he deflected. "Give me your keys!" she commanded. Olo ripped the keys out of his hand before dragging him by the collar to her own car, shoving him in the front seat and yelling back at the girls, "You skank bitches get your own stinky pussies home!"

Olo tore out of the driveway, and roared away with tires screeching. Both girls came in the house for several awkward minutes, until a rideshare picked them up, thus ending this unorthodox Christmas-In-the-Manger episode.

***

When Jordan and Maria woke up on Christmas morning, Bill's car was gone, and they did not hear from either again, nor did they call, though it was discussed. Both felt fortunate nothing bad happened even though they went to the edge of the unknown for them, and they weren't wanting to push that envelope another hair. Jordan's superstition still held, a belief that he could experience his share of suffering or adversity in life vicariously, and he learned enough from the mistakes of others to avoid making more whoppers of his own. While he still made his share of mistakes, he knew enough when to stop and once with Olo was enough. They were just praying there wasn't any more to it.

***

But six months later, Jordan and Olo crossed paths again. He was leaving the hospital after visiting a sick friend when

Olo sneaked up from behind to surprise him, and whispered, "Don't make me squeal, you fucker."

Jordan wheeled around to face her huge blue eyes dead-on. As always they were intense with their size and aliveness and his mouth opened in a lustful gasp on recognition. Olo's chest moved in and out fast. They almost hugged until he saw she was pregnant.

"Oh, Olo, well…" he stammered, almost congratulating her on the pregnancy but hesitating for some reason.

"So what are you doing at the hospital?" she asked right away. "Everything is alright?"

"Oh, yes, visiting a friend," he replied. "I have only one strange belief, well, it's really a superstition. If I visit or help people who are having troubles, I'll have *less* of my own."

"Hah! You are kidding!"

"No, no, it works for me."

"You are funny!" she exclaimed. "I, too, have a strange superstition. Maybe I shouldn't say!" She laughed. "Mine is the opposite, if I am around people who have troubles, then I would have even more troubles!" Olo gave him a light hug of her own accord. "So, how are you and Maria? I don't blame you for not staying in touch. That was some time we all had, yes?" she spoke rhetorically.

"You said it!" They laughed. She was around six months along, raising his concerns about having come inside her. He almost mentioned the baby again, but didn't. "Yes, Olo, we felt real good. An unforgettable experience with you… And, umm, Bill." They exchanged smiles. "My wife and I secretly dreamed of doing something adventurous like that. So, with you, it was much more than we had even hoped for. We were so thankful, too." He almost gagged on the triteness.

"Oh, yes, unforgettable, that was. Thank you! Well, yes, it is true what Bill said, we got a lot out of our systems!"

"Nobody got hurt, either, that was also real good!" They laughed nervously. "So, Olo, you got pregnant since we saw you, congratulations. You stayed with Bill? What happened?"

She whipped out a glossy flyer of herself in pointy-tail devil's costume with leather dominatrix harness and bulging pregnant, yet wielding a pitchfork and whip over a thin hairy slave kneeling with a bondage helmet locked on his head.

"There is my Bill!" she said proudly. "That's our big act! We are paid for the 'Dark Devil' shows, do you believe it? Yes, you know, it is a big subculture, devil worship. People misunderstand. We don't believe in *real* devils. It only means indulgence and gratifications of all kinds, like any consensual fantasies. But goes against today's 'gods' like the greed, and oppression. But, it's all good. Bill plays his part well, that is true. I let the girls play with him. He lets me flirt or play with the other boys." She had more nervous giggles for him. "Not like we did!"

"Oh, no, well, of course not!" he played along. "Actually nothing wrong with the 'extra' pleasures, like we had!" But, the whole thing looked too weird for him. It was impossible to relate to the real Olo, or Bill for that matter. Again, Jordan considered the possibilities of disease in such a freewheeling culture of sketchy risk-takers, so now he wasn't just worried about her pregnancy, but whether he or Maria may also have something communicable. He resolved to get the answers he wanted with direct questions, inquiring, "You look great! All good, then, with you? And the baby? Just here for a wellness check?"

"Yes. We are both good. Both very healthy. So far!" She laughed. "Bill is fine, too. We will say Hello for you!"

"I'm happy you two got back together… After all that."

"Yes. I do love my Bill. As you must know, I like to be on top!" She laughed heartily. "Yes, we must confess!" And, her face spread out in a joyful expression with the ice-blue eyes popping forth.

Olo had what she wanted, but she knew it, too! She was happy with that, and Jordan was happy for them. They were perfect for the sort of lives they wanted to share, and perfect for the magical evening he and Maria wanted to share. Love had no other way to go for them all. It was one of the times a person thinks about life, Perfect Is How Things Are! Then comes the realization that while perfection sounds great and oftentimes it was, perfection didn't necessarily mean people liked what happened or that it was going to be nice. Jordan's odd superstition led him here as well as the bar on Christmas Eve, while the striking resemblance to Olo's rapist father was in twisted ways, a catalyst for all their pleasure, and Maria's secret fantasies facilitated everything else. Who people were at any given time determined their choices, so events did not have any other way to come together for people than the way they do come together. Plus, no one knows precisely what the "coming together" will look like or where it leads; it is chains of choices and effects, opening infinite possibilities between all people and things, but all with their own equally "perfect" outcomes.

He was about to share his minor revelation with Olo and she might even agree, but bringing up her abuse here was one of those bad choices. Besides seeing Olo again reminded him mostly of his happiness with Maria, only making him prouder of the extra-special relationship they continued to build. How many in the world kept feeling better and better about the one they are with for 25 years? Not that many, he guessed. More than anything he wanted to get home and back into that total comfort and trust with each other, making love to his wife 'til she glowed in the dark.

When he got home everything was still. He had to wait.

Because of Olo, he recalled having to wait when he got home from the bar on Christmas Eve, but unlike that night six months ago, the thought occurred to him, Perfect was *always* how it is, whether people noticed it, or they liked it, or not!

***

Half-hour later Maria unlocked the door, all fresh-faced and cheerful with her familiar hair bun rounding out the soft curves of her cheeks and forehead. Also, perhaps due to Olo he seemed to consider his wife with new eyes, and didn't see a single thing he didn't love including her "little" flaws which had acquired a strangely endearing quality over time.

She began with a small laugh. "Well, you won't guess who called out of the blue a few minutes ago?"

He smiled wide. "First, you have to guess who I ran into at the hospital!"

They shared the answer without words, and that was all there was between them concerning Olo, and Bill. Again, he recognized how Maria meant most everything to his life, his one true fantasy lover. She had disagreeable moments—him more than her! And, though not a classic beauty-pageant face and hair, she turned him on in a flash, better than any woman imaginable, quick as a hiccup, or bunnies on a hot date. His wild fantasy lover nicely packaged into the Real Deal. Their relationship was almost too good to be true, he thought; still, there it was! In fact, given the necessary trust, attention and mutual respect, he saw nothing too impossible about it! And could well happen for almost anyone!

He got this overwhelming urge to kiss and hold her, and when she looked at him a pleasing glimmer also shone in her eyes. They joined for one of their quiet and slow embraces, rocking in a soft dance rhythm of their own heartbeats, with kissing, caresses and lightly feeling one another's figure. He cuddled the notches under her cushy breast folds, while Maria responded by surging up through her chest, to pull him closer and harder into her so that her breasts dragged along the full length of his forearms. They breathed lightly on each other's face and neck.

It was all about their comfortable reliable connection, a gift they cherished and relished. Both realized the incredible specialness of their loving brand, the tender concrete of their lives, appreciating everything together about that one person right now, this place, and this one time in the universe which completed who they were by making each of them whole.

Hearts and breaths quickened, passions taking off when

Maria squeaked little, "Oo-oooh…" and, "Aa-aah…" noises in his ear that tingled way down through his tippy-toes. "Oo-oh…" She whispered, "You're gonna make me squeal, o-oh, yes." It was Maria's sexiest little voice. "Yes, daddy-boy, like that…there. Yeah."

Jordan crushed his chest into hers with strong engulfing arms and forceful fingers creasing her supple back, and sides.

"Like that…"

"Like always…"

They kissed, and kept kissing.

"The one and only…for me."

More kisses.

"One sure thing in the universe…"

"No probability about that."

"Glad I gambled on you."

"Glad I gambled on *you*…"

"We braved all the possible dangers…"

"Risked all the unknowns together."

"To win the top prize."

"The biggest prize in the world…"

"Just this."

"That's us."

"That's it."

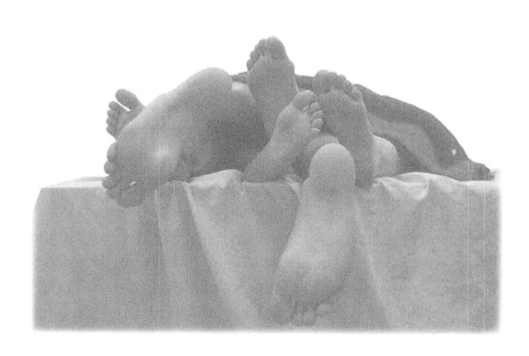

Six Feet of Tender Concrete

Afterword

Our Fates, Chances and Free Will

Taking one's beliefs and behavior to extreme limits before somehow finding the safest edge from which to conduct their lives, is a vital skill the people in these stories were able to negotiate for their long-term benefits. Whether helped by luck, karma, Providence or by making better choices, a great majority of us prefer *not* to believe things will just happen with no purpose or discernable cause. While these characters were driven by overwhelming urges plus ignorance to go far beyond what is reasonable and rational risk-taking, all barely "survive" to head off with changed worldviews; and, though helplessly compelled to do what they did before skirting the most dire consequences, none were predestined to end up the way they do. The subtle difference makes all the difference.

In this world which appears to operate by causation, we see patterns and assign responsibility, among other reasons to prove or disprove the notion of "determinism" where, in the final analysis, all things are "fated" to wind up how they do. By extension, such thinking means that events are fated to go "any old way," or even, "how God *wants* them to go," since those fatalistic belief systems also give up responsibility and control over the outcomes, reducing free will to delusion and living to an exercise of going through motions.

When indulging their desires develops into compulsion or rages uncontrolled, it wreaks havoc on lives too. Catalyst of the main character's indulgent behavior in the first story is materialism, money for toys, pursuing what looks good and he thinks will make him feel good. Whereas the character in the second story is tempted to overindulge what her physical body craves by pursuing too much hedonistic desire, people in the third and fourth story are also tempted by materialism and hedonism, but mostly they are victims of over-indulging their profound egoism, and needing to achieve a certain status at least in their own eyes.

Whether these people were born with or developed their weaknesses along the way, their weaknesses exist before they succumb to the urges and temptations which landed them in danger. While not "destined," per se, they were bound to run into precipitating situations during the course of living, and primed to make the dubious choices they were bound to make in the stories. They also have opportunities to arrive at better choices and prevent more catastrophic damage to their lives, but they were not predestined as much as "pre-primed" to go off the rails, and to barely avoid oblivion as well.

Their compulsion to satisfy evermore risky desires and push the limits of indulgence for the sake of indulging, may conjure "satanic" overtones, but the takeaway should be that all action invokes risk or uncertainty or action would not be called for, and whether we act or not, we are in the reality of potentials and probability, risk or taking chances, be it a new friend, job, trip to the store or straight to the casino. We "bet" on outcomes with assumptions, often using minimal thought and bank on them to work out how we expect, spending our days weighing the odds against plus the risks of action (or nonaction) we believe further our interests, and satisfaction. We might not press our luck at the blackjack table, but risk-reward predictions dictate our choice-making. The potential pain of loss became too great for these characters when they used any strength they had left to stop it, then kept choosing that despite unyielding contrary forces.

Thus, we battle to reconcile the cold statistical certainty of probability with fate and free will, saying such things as, It's Providence, or, It is fated, or, The world is too wondrous to have happened by chance. Still, Einstein was wrong about this one, God doesn't just play dice with the world, it would seem He *only* plays dice with the world! God may stand for and BE ALL PROBABILITIES! Which is exactly how we exist—a place where things like us could be happening now must occur at least once throughout the cosmos, so we do.

Since every photon of energy exists in its quantum state with the potential to be a particle or wave until observed, such as when it strikes a sensor or otherwise interacts with us, we can't consider such-and-such to be fate, or "how God wants it" until we know the presumably fated outcome; but by then it is mere hindsight, and colored by our countless beliefs and biases! An outcome doesn't exist until the final nanoseconds when all the other photons, matter and energy in that cosmic neighborhood coalesce before us to make events—only then can it be interpreted as fated, destined, etc. So, whether what happens in the stories should be called coincidence, destiny, Providence, it's a moot question since we never know 100% what outcomes will be even if we have full control, and free will does exist, and all the probabilities are stacked one way.

The Universe itself might not be able to plan and predict outcomes 100%, but the fact that probabilities exist and make zillion-to-one odds uncertain (gamblers can feel this in their bones) means there is also "enough play" in our universe for free will to exist, and on some level to influence whether any possible result happens on earth. Probabilities must exist for us to use, too, however small or illusory their influence is.

These characters had as much of the "gambler" in them as anybody, and at times their compulsions did rage full blast albeit temporarily. They never took on those compulsions as identities, though, not giving up their whole lives to them as essential elements or reasons for being.

Unnecessary reckless actions as a basic element of one's being, like crime, gambling or unhealthy living, is less about escaping reality than *negating* reality, disproving its validity or power over their lives; so they ignore or buck heavy odds against self-defeating choices, and normalize bad fortune by rationalizing, "Things screw up, sure… But, I still live to win my thrilling chances, addicted to these pure adrenalin shots of excitement and win-or-bust fright with my being at risk; it's life on the edge of our personal hot seat, tapping my own pipeline to the universe that gets me over the odds, and I can finally conquer my fears of losing or oblivion to be the one who could beat all the odds in the end! The Comeback Kid! So, it's like, I'm ready to take my chances almost any time. Maybe I am nuts, I don't know. And, I do win. Sometimes."

For those with related self-narratives, we may say they are "fated" to continue hurting their prospects for happiness, as fate itself is defined by such fatalism. The characters fall short of similar hardened or compulsive self-narratives. Yet, even destinies and fate call for some measure of fulfillment, with an element of choosing and commitment to its fulfilling. The characters build on who they are before their crises and in the end create the openings that allow for whatever cosmic purposes they were presented, or meant to fill, to be fulfilled.

By the world working how it does in these stories and in our lives, and we can rely on that, the *only sure thing* on and near our planet's surface, is how *nothing is certain* or much less fated, unless it already exists and its probabilities don't.

Inside the earth, or out in the universe where the human will exerts no influence yet, incomprehensible lethal powers determine the course of everything else. We take our chances with all those! Which doesn't mean they won't be predicted, controlled and avoided sometime to curb their perils. Without those inherently lethal potentials we can't control, there's no reward as our existence is but one outcome along an endless continuum of potentialities.

While incomprehensible forces forever dominate all the other natural phenomena or cycles charting our beings, their inexplicable evolution into a self-balancing cause-and-effect universe that expands with infinite potentials, permeates this world through its eternal influencing. Such balancing forces keep dictating 99.99% of our circumstances from billions of light years away. They fuel our chances and choices moment to moment, infuse humanity's dreams, and forever drive our instinctual quests to solve and evolve as we dodge extinction from countless threats, always shooting to beat even the most impossible odds against us.

About the Author

Originally a New Yorker, René Blanco grew up in New England, studied writing at UCLA and lives in Ocean Ridge, Florida. He's been producing notable scripts, fast fiction and novels while living another rewarding life as a therapist and child advocate. His TV and film achievements include screenplays for NBC's long-running "Third Watch" series, and the global action-thriller, "Noah's Descendants."

Blanco's first story collection, *PLEASURE ON THE RUN*, enjoyed its debut at The Miami Book Fair International, and a newly expanded edition containing bonus materials, titled *FIGHT AND FLIGHT (Moments of Truth and Do or Die Tales)*, is also available under the *FlightBooks™* publishing banner. Another acclaimed book, *ADULT STORIES,* is succeeded here by this equally dynamic and provocative work, *INDULGENCE OR GRATIFICATIONS,* about people discovering the limits and risks of various temptations, and excites the fancy of readers with classic *FlightBooks™* qualities—powerful throughout and criss-crosses the map of human experience!

Other new *FlightBooks* include, *APPETIZERS FOR THE APOCALYPSE (Post-COVID Tales About Foreseeable Unknowns)*, *BANNED BOOK (Forbidden Tales of Fetish, Revolt and Taboo)*, plus *ANTIGRAVITY (Fantastical Tales of Higher Importance)!*

Excerpts from published works, including reviews along with his works in progress, are posted on the author website, reneblanco.net, where signed *FlightBooks™* are always one of the most meaningful, fun, inexpensive gift choices ever!

Conclusion

"Reason obscures *The Infinite* but
I still live in your unconscious."

— from a dream of Dr. Ironicus

Made in the USA
Columbia, SC
16 April 2023

14826515R00088